"What's wrong, hon?" he asked in a hoarse voice. **"Why are we stopping?"**

"Because it's not a good idea. We shouldn't be doing this."

"Why not?"

"Because I work for you. It could get uncomfortable."

"To hell with uncomfortable. Tell me you don't like what I'm doing."

His lips grazed the side of her neck, nipping and sucking. She was pulsing all over, uncontrollably.

Kennedy's fingers dug into Salim's back, squeezing and kneading the hard muscles. His hands were on her butt now, bringing her closer to him until she could feel his hardness and hear his raspy breaths in her ear. The feel and smell of him excited her.

"I want to make love to you," he said gruffly.

"We shouldn't."

MARCIA KING-GAMBLE

is a national bestselling author, and a former travel-industry executive. She's lived in five different states and has traveled to some of the more exotic parts of the world. The Far East, Venice and New Zealand are still her favorites.

She enjoys a good workout, is passionate about animals, old houses and tearjerker movies. Marcia is also the editor of a monthly newsletter entitled *Marcia's Romantically Yours.* Log on to her Web site, www.lovemarcia.com, and find out what she's all about.

Marcia King-Gamble
TEMPTING
MOGUL
the

KIMANI™
ROMANCE

This one's for Shanna Eilers—
my Pacific Northwest Connection and breakfast pal.

 KIMANI PRESS™

PLEASE RECYCLE
THIS PRODUCT IS RECYCLABLE

ISBN-13: 978-0-373-86093-7
ISBN-10:   0-373-86093-5

Recycling programs
for this product may
not exist in your area.

TEMPTING THE MOGUL

www.kimanipress.com

Printed in U.S.A.

Dear Reader,

Seattle has always been a favorite city, and even though I've traveled the world, it still remains one of my top-ten places. It just might have something to do with me landing there right out of flight-attendant school back in the day.

Last year I had the opportunity to return to this city for an extended period of time. I found much had changed, yet my love affair began all over again. Seattle is simply the kind of place that calls to you because of its beauty and tolerance of different lifestyles.

Therefore you can only imagine how excited I was to pen a series set in this wonderful city. My biggest challenge was crafting my heroine's personality because she is organized, orderly and totally unemotional—very different from me. I had fun with the whole process of her becoming unraveled when she fell in love.

If you've enjoyed reading this book, keep in mind there are two more books in the Get a Life series. I am currently working on the second. While you're waiting, consider taking a little vacation, and put Seattle on your list. You'll fall in love with the Emerald City just as I have.

Romantically yours,

Marcia King-Gamble

Chapter 1

"Hey, where are you going with my car?" Kennedy Fitzgerald shouted, racing after the tow truck backing out of her driveway that had her precious Honda attached; the Honda she planned on paying off in full next week.

A few tendrils escaped the headband Kennedy had used to pull her hair back. In a frustrated motion she swept them off her face before flailing her arms at the driver. "You have no right to take my car! I've been making monthly payments!"

The tow truck driver spotting her came to a halt. He wound down his window and peered out. "Look, lady, I'm just doing my job. Pay your car note and the finance company won't repossess your car. It's the way things work."

"Pay my note? What are you talking about?" Kennedy shouted. She could feel her face heating up. "I pay my bills on time, way before they're due. Why am I explaining this to you?"

"Tell the story to the bank. Don't beat up the messenger."

Through his open window the driver flipped her a business card. It floated to the ground. As Kennedy bent to retrieve it he floored the accelerator, and zoomed off with her vehicle attached.

"Miss, you owe me forty-five dollars," the cabdriver who'd been unloading her luggage carped. He'd been watching the action from a safe distance.

Kennedy let out a deep sigh and peeled off a few bills, folding them into the man's open palm. Wait until she got her hands on her cousin Marna. How could she let this happen?

"Can I have a receipt?" Kennedy asked the driver.

He fumbled through several piles of paper and found a preprinted receipt. *Where is Marna anyway?* Why hadn't she come out to greet her and help her unload? She had to have heard the taxi pull up, or at the very least the noisy tow truck.

Marna had been living with Kennedy rent free. In exchange for not paying rent, she'd agreed to take care of the triplex and collect the rent from the other apartments. This money was to be used to pay Kennedy's bills while she was gone—including the car note.

To make it easier for the money to be deposited, Kennedy had asked her tenants to write checks directly to Marna. She'd instructed her to collect the rent checks on the first of the month from each tenant and deposit them in the joint account they'd opened up.

Knowing that a real person was responsible for collecting checks and depositing the money in an account had given Kennedy peace of mind. She'd left for her assignment in Tokyo feeling confident that her bills would be paid and her house cared for. For six months she'd been coaching Japanese executives on how business was done in America. She'd taught the Japanese everything from social etiquette to how to dress. The position had come with an attractive salary, plus housing. It had also come at exactly the right time.

The Fortune 500 company Kennedy had been working for was downsizing like crazy. When a headhunter called, she'd eagerly listened to his sales pitch. She was single with no dependents, and had a dual master's in Japanese and industrial psychology. *Why not?*

All in all, not many thirty-year-old African-Americans got a sweet deal like that. Kennedy had it all planned out. When she returned to Seattle she'd go into business for herself. She'd hang out a shingle advertising her services as a bilingual life coach and corporate trainer.

The sky was an unusual blue for Seattle. Cerulean blue, instead of blue-gray. A cool breeze ruffled the budding trees and in the distance, Kennedy saw the snowcapped mountain peaks she'd missed so much and loved to hike.

She stabbed a finger at the buzzer and waited for Marna to come bounding down the stairs and help her with all her bags. Finally, growing impatient, she let herself in through the side entrance.

Behind her, even though it was the end of May, the tulips were still in full bloom. The yard outside the triplex needed weeding and she wondered why Marna hadn't called the gardener as she'd been told to do.

"Do you need a hand?" a male voice asked, behind her.

Kennedy turned to find her downstairs tenant—a techie type—eyeing her curiously. "Yes, Ed, that would be great."

"How was your trip?" he asked, scooping up two of her bags as if they weighed nothing.

"Long, but I got a lot of work done so that was good."

"You liked working with Japanese businesspeople?"

Kennedy tried not to yawn. Jet lag was quickly setting in and she was in no mood for stupid questions. "Loved it. I got to use both my Japanese and organizational development skills. It was fun teaching American business protocol."

Kennedy started up the stairs to her apartment

carrying the lightest of the suitcases. Underfoot in the foyer and hallways the Berber carpets were stained and smelly. She did not own a dog, but there was a definite 'doggie' scent to the place.

Ed snorted and filled her in. "Wow! That rottie your cousin had in here really wasn't toilet trained."

Her head began to ache. "What rottie?"

One of her strengths was remaining cool, calm and collected. She taught people how to cope with unexpected life-changing events. Therefore she should easily be able to deal with this.

"Marna's dog, Lulu," Ed said. "I told her the dog was bored and needed toys."

"Since when does Marna have a dog?" Kennedy threw over her shoulder.

Ed shrugged. "Oops! Talk about open mouth and insert foot. Lulu's a stray Marna found wandering the streets. She's a sweetheart but totally untrained. She ran Marna."

Kennedy sucked in a breath while using the green key to unlock the top lock. "Where is Marna anyway?"

"Uh, didn't she call you?"

Kennedy narrowed her eyes and again looked at Ed. Mentally she counted to ten. "Why would Marna need to call me? She knew when I was coming home. I e-mailed her."

"Did she e-mail you back? That's better than what she's been doing to me."

Come to think of it, Marna hadn't responded but Kennedy had thought nothing of it. Her cousin was notoriously scatterbrained and always acted as if she was overwhelmed.

Ed set down Kennedy's two bags. "You should be good to go from here."

"Uh-uh. Not until you tell me what you know."

Ed was beet red. He wore the uncomfortable expression of a man caught between rock and granite. He shuffled from one foot to another.

"Ed," Kennedy groused. "Better fess up if you know what's good for you. Seattle's rentals are pretty steep and you've got a great deal as my tenant."

Ed exhaled loudly. "Never thought you'd be a fan of bribery. Marna's been gone for almost three months. Some kind of an emergency came up and she had to leave."

Kennedy's throat closed down. She tried to control the wheezing sounds coming from her nose and the buzzing in her ears. She was close to hyperventilating. "Then how on earth have you and the Dopwells on the second floor been paying your rent?"

"Marna told us to send the rent to a P.O. box."

"What! Better give me that box number."

"No problem, I'll get it to you."

Kennedy's temples were pounding. She could not allow herself to get out of control. There had to be a logical explanation to it all. She kept thinking of her silver car that had just been repossessed. *Was the triplex that she'd saved so hard to buy on the brink of foreclosure, too? How many months late was everything anyway?* She'd need to call the bank immediately.

The minute she pushed open her top-floor apartment door, Kennedy knew she had her hands full. A damp, stagnant odor almost knocked her over. The rottweiler had left her mark here, as well. Kennedy flipped on the lights and braced herself. The suitcase she was holding fell from her limp fingers, making a dull thud. She felt Ed's steadying hands on her shoulders as she surveyed the destruction.

"Sit and I'll get you a glass of water," he proposed.

Unable to answer him, Kennedy just gaped. Her beautiful place was in ruins. The Persian carpets were a mess and the sofa she was still paying for had ugly yellow markings. She shuddered thinking about what those stains were. Her lovely wooden floors were scratched. The baseboards and moldings had been chewed on.

No wonder Marna had bailed before Kennedy came home and killed her.

Ed lined up the suitcases in the foyer and hastily opened up windows. A cool spring breeze soon filled the interior. It wasn't enough to camouflage the smell.

"Airing the place out should help," he announced, his voice chipper. "It'll be too much for you to do alone but tomorrow you can call a cleaning service."

Kennedy exhaled loudly and willed herself to calm

down. She'd been named after John F. Kennedy, the thirty-fifth president of the United States, and a man her mother thought walked on water. She'd liked that he promoted equal rights and world peace. But Kennedy's thoughts right now were anything but peaceful.

"I can stick around and help you straighten up," Ed offered.

"You've done enough. Just get me that mailbox address and I'll take it from here." She thanked him and walked with him to the door.

"I really don't mind helping," Ed insisted. "In fact I would be glad to do what I can."

"You're sweet, but no. I need to do this alone."

After he left Kennedy wandered through what she playfully called her penthouse, assessing and itemizing the damage. Many of her personal possessions would have to be dumped. They'd been either chewed or soiled on. She began a list of things she needed to do first thing tomorrow.

She'd need to call someone in to clean the carpet in the bedroom and the living room's upholstery. She'd have to find someone to look at the wooden floors and see what could be done about them.

Kennedy glanced at the blinking answering machine. All of her friends and family knew that she'd been in Tokyo. They knew how to reach her via e-mail or cell phone. She'd entrusted her cousin on her mother's side, to house sit and pay her bills. Marna was between jobs and needed a place to live. She seemed grateful for the small income Kennedy was willing to pay.

Kennedy had had some trepidation about turning over a responsible job like collecting rent, and bill paying to a flake. She would have much preferred her brothers to take on the task, but Lincoln lived in Eastern Washington, too far away to be tracking down rent checks, or so he'd said. He had a brand new baby and didn't have the time or inclination to be playing landlord.

Roosevelt who lived in Edmonds, much closer, had urged Kennedy to give Marna a chance. He was holding down two jobs and felt he had a roof over his head and an income coming in. Marna didn't. He'd also promised to keep an eye on their cousin. Given what had gone down that hadn't happened. Marna had botched the job that she'd claimed she badly needed. Now she'd turned Kennedy's orderly life into a nightmare. Why, oh why, hadn't she listened to her gut?

Kennedy was so angry she jabbed the answering machine's rewind button with more force than she intended. Surprisingly, the machine wasn't full and the few calls recorded were from telemarketers. Toward the end there was one call that made her pause.

She rewound it, listening carefully. A woman iden-tified herself as Diane, the assistant to the president of TSW Studios, wanted Kennedy to return her call ASAP.

What would a television station want with me? Yes,

she'd heard of Tanner Washington, the studio's owner, but she and he didn't move in the same circles. He was notoriously low profile and never even allowed himself to be photographed. Kennedy had never seen him. Curiosity prompted Kennedy to scribble down the number. She'd call Diane tomorrow.

Jet lag was beginning to kick in when Kennedy made her phone call to the bank where she had her mortgage. She navigated the voice activation maze and finally got a living, breathing person.

"Ms. Fitzpatrick," a stern-sounding service representative said, "you're two months late on your mortgage. In another month you'll be in foreclosure."

Even though she'd been expecting something like this, the cold hand of fear grabbed her heart. She was so angry she could spit. Her precious triplex that she loved, and had worked her butt off to buy, was in danger of being sold to someone else.

Kennedy started to ramble and make excuses, then caught herself. The representative didn't need to hear her problems, nor did she care.

"What will it take to get current?" she asked quickly.

The woman named a figure. Kennedy did some mental calculations. She should have enough in her savings to make that payment and bring her mortgage up to date. She also had a rather hefty check in her purse. She'd insisted that the Japanese pay her in U.S. dollars, and she'd planned on depositing that check tomorrow. She'd just need to find some way to get to the bank.

Her world was toppling down around her and it seemed as though there was nothing she could do to stop it. She'd tossed the tow truck driver's card in her purse. His company would be the next place to call. She needed wheels to take care of business and get her life back in order.

"Is there anything else I can help you with?" the customer service representative asked, reminding Kennedy she was still on the line.

"Can you take my mortgage payment over the phone? Will that payment register today?"

"I'll have to transfer you to our account services department," the woman said, sounding smooth as silk. "As you know your account is delinquent."

Forty minutes later, Kennedy finally hung up with the credit manager. It had taken some explaining, even pleading, but at least she was now paid to date. She'd coughed up the money for the hefty finance and late charges, but she was certain that her credit score had taken a beating. It would take years for her to rebuild good credit.

Several months of rent checks, money she'd counted on to take care of her bills, had disappeared along with Marna. The excess money she'd hoped to have in her bank account would now be used up to pay off delinquent bills. She'd thought she was doing a good deed helping Marna. What was the saying? No good deed went unpunished.

Kennedy's head continued to pound as she punched in the number for Joe's Towing. She was placed on an interminable hold only to have an automated voice tell her she was calling outside regular business hours.

"Dammit!" she muttered, hanging up.

As she was close to tossing the receiver across the room, the phone rang in her hand.

"Hello?" she tried not to growl.

"Yes, I need Kennedy Fitzgerald, please?" a female voice she didn't recognize said.

"This is she," Kennedy said. *Please let it not be a creditor.*

"Ms. Fitzgerald, I'm Diane, assistant to Tanner Washington, the president of TSW Studios. He's been hoping to speak to you."

Trying to make up for her less than friendly greeting, Kennedy said, "Can you tell me what this is about?"

"Mr. Washington would prefer to discuss the issue in person. He learned through a source that you're back in town. Since the matter is of some urgency, he's wondering if you could meet him at the studio tomorrow morning, say around eleven?"

Midmorning would give Kennedy enough time to go to the bank and contact the towing company again. Maybe she would even have a car.

"I'll be there," she answered, then hung up.

* * *

Bright and early the next morning, Kennedy tried calling the company that had towed her car. She kept being transferred from one area to another, and then decided it might be in her best interest to just show up in person. The challenge now was to rent a car. She called several automobile rental companies until she found one willing to pick her up at home. When she attempted to reserve the vehicle her credit card was turned down.

"How could that be?" she asked the rental agent.

"I don't know, ma'am, it just says declined and I've run it through several times."

Another call to the credit card's customer service department revealed her bill hadn't been paid in months. The account was canceled. Yet another strike against Marna.

Desperate, Kennedy used her bank debit card to reserve the vehicle. She was on her way and had a small measure of peace.

Her first stop was at Puget Sound Mutual, the bank that financed her car and where she did her personal banking. After she'd explained what had happened over and over, a sympathetic bank clerk took her to see one of the vice presidents. By then Kennedy was through talking and very close to crying.

She really was going to knock Marna out when she got her hands on her. She would have been better off trusting her tenants with her bank routing number and having them make their own deposits. She wouldn't have this headache now if she'd paid her bills electronically. But no, she's thought it best that someone closer to home pick up her rent checks and pay her bills. What a mistake that had been.

The bank's records showed they'd made numerous attempts to contact Kennedy and work out arrangements. Hearing nothing back, they'd repossessed the car.

Kennedy explained her situation and the officer expressed sympathy and made several phone calls, but to no avail. The vehicle was most likely being auctioned as they spoke.

By then the headache had become a migraine. How on earth would she get from Bellevue to downtown Seattle in twenty minutes? If there was traffic on the bridge she was toast.

Driving like a speed demon, Kennedy managed to make it into the parking lot of TSW Studios with five minutes to spare. She used that time to comb her hair, shove her headband back in place and apply fresh lip gloss. She'd never been much for makeup and no one would ever describe her as trendy. Kennedy's clothing was always more functional than stylish.

Once inside, she handed her ID to the guard at the desk in the lobby and waited for Diane to come and get her. Five minutes into her wait a thirty-something, athletically built man came sauntering in.

He was the kind of African-American male who, although casually dressed, turned heads. His hunter-green flannel shirt stretched across his broad chest, and was tucked into baggy jeans that slouched at the knees. His scuffed boots looked as though they'd seen better days. Although his overall appearance shouted *mountain man,* there was a sensuality and confidence to him that was very appealing.

He approached the guard's circular desk and flicked a finger at him. "Morning, Andrew. How's it going?"

The guard, who'd been hunched over his station with an eye on the newspaper, folded it quickly and gave him his full attention. "Good morning, Mr. Washington. It's been a long time! How was safari?"

This couldn't be Tanner Washington. Kennedy was expecting someone much older.

"Please call me Salim, Andrew. Mr. Washington is my father," the man who looked as if he could straddle Mount Rainier in one leap corrected. "Zimbabwe was incredible. Just a beautiful country, but no safari for me. Just my usual humanitarian work for two months."

"What I wouldn't give to visit Africa," the guard said, longingly.

"The Peace Corps might be the way to go. You'd be doing something worthy while at the same time ex-periencing a new country. I signed up for a two-year stint after graduating college. Since then it's been very difficult for me to stay in one place for any length of time. Is Mr. Washington around?"

"I didn't see him leave."

Salim's complexion was the color of raw brown sugar and his eyes were equally as light. He did a quick scan of the lobby as if expecting his father to jump out from behind one of the potted ficus plants. His glance rested briefly on Kennedy and she was treated to a warm smile that began at the corner of his tawny eyes and settled in his square jaw. She liked his full lips and the way his mouth turned up at the corners. He looked as though he laughed a lot.

"Who do we have here?" he said loud enough for Kennedy to hear him, turning back to the guard.

She didn't hear the guard's response. Probably just as well, she didn't need some wealthy playboy flirting with her right before she had a meeting with his father. Her priority was getting back her car and she would focus on that once this meeting was over.

The petite, smartly dressed woman who came bustling out of the elevator must be the studio head's assistant. When she approached the guard, Mountain Man swept her off her feet.

"Di, you look younger than ever," he gushed.

"Put me down!" she said, chuckling. "I don't have time for this nonsense. Though I am glad you're back. We'll talk later. I'm here to collect your father's visitor," the assistant said.

Salim Washington set Diane back on her feet.

The guard pointed to Kennedy and the petite woman came mincing over.

"Ms. Fitzgerald," she said. "I'm Diane, Mr. Washington's assistant. Have you been waiting long?"

"No, your timing is perfect."

Kennedy looked over at Salim and he was no longer the smiling, affable guy who'd come sauntering through the lobby. He threw her a thunderous look of surprise and what looked like—no, it couldn't be—disgust.

What was that *all about?* No time to psychoanalyze now, the television mogul was waiting.

Chapter 2

Salim would rather be anywhere but here. TSW Studios was a place he'd avoided like the plague. It was much too artificial an environment for him. But the old man's assistant had called acting as if it was a life-and-death situation and because it was Diane, and he liked Diane, he'd dropped everything to come.

He was not here for the man who called himself his father, that was for sure. He wasn't interested in anything that philanderer had to say.

His father, Tanner Washington's autocratic approach to everyone in his life had turned Salim off. They were worlds apart in the way they conducted business and dealt with people.

Salim's mother, Lucinda, had also called Salim telling him to go see his father. She was the peacemaker in the family and she'd finally persuaded him to hear the old man out. His self-suffering mother was the most wonderful woman in the world and he would do almost anything she asked, even meet with a man he disliked intensely.

He'd made one hour for Tanner Washington. So far that whole hour had been taken up by the young African-American woman with the Asian cast to her features. She was the woman who'd been seated in the lobby, the one he'd thought was very attractive.

More than attractive actually. More like beautiful, in a wholesome but classy sort of way. In an era where tats, weaves, piercings, bling and barely there clothing were in vogue, this woman, who wore minimal makeup and a conservative hairstyle, stood out. Salim had been especially intrigued by the outfit: a classic navy suit worn with sensible pumps and pearls. She certainly didn't seem the type to work in a television studio, more likely a bank.

As the minutes ticked by, he was getting more and more irritated. She'd been behind closed doors with his father for far too long. He had places to go and people to see. *What exactly are they doing in there anyway?*

"Di, how much longer will he be?" Salim quizzed the old man's assistant. It took a lot to address the old goat by "father." An adulterer did not deserve that kind of respect.

"I scheduled his interview for an hour," Diane answered in her usual, unperturbed manner. "If I'd known you were planning to pop in, I would have booked you time." She lowered her glasses, looking at him.

Salim winked at Diane. "If you can fit me in I'll take you to lunch, you gorgeous thing."

"I can buy my own lunch, thanks. Save your flirting for that string of wide-eyed young things your own age that you impress with stories of your travels."

He wished there was a string of young things. Lately he'd had no time for romantic entanglements, not even flings.

"You're a hard woman, Di," Salim said, clutching his heart. "One day you just might succumb to my charm. You know you're a cougar in a fab suit."

Diane settled her glasses back on her nose and gave him the full effect of her cold, unsettling stare. "I don't think so. I like my men buttoned down and settled. I'm too old to babysit."

Salim chuckled. He absolutely loved the woman and her droll sense of humor.

She was one of those ageless matrons who must have been a knockout in her heyday. Diane was the complete package: efficient, good looking, intellectual and fearless. She took no guff from her tyrannical boss, which was another reason Tanner kept her around. As studio head he was used to intimidating people. Diane simply could not be intimidated.

Salim hovered at Diane's circular desk, listening shamelessly while she buzzed her boss.

"Your son's been waiting to see you for almost an hour," she said in an even voice that never changed, even when Tanner was having a hissy fit, which was often.

When Diane's eyebrows rose a fraction, Salim guessed the old man's response wasn't exactly positive. Not that that came as a big surprise.

"You've got about fifteen minutes free after you're through with Ms. Fitzgerald," Diane reminded the mogul. "And you did have me call Salim earlier this week. You said you wanted to see him."

Salim tapped the face of his Timex and whispered to Diane, "Tell your boss I have to be somewhere in forty minutes. Never mind, I'll tell him myself."

"Salim!"

He ignored her and strode toward the closed office door.

"You can't just go bursting in on an interview," Diane called after him.

"Watch me. My time is just as valuable as his."

He paused briefly in front of the smoked-glass double doors that had Tanner Washington, President of TSW engraved on them. The T stood for Tanner and the S for Salim. It had never occurred to the pompous old ass to make it TSCW and include his daughter Christiane's initials.

Tanner's dream had been that one day his son would

take over from him. Except Salim couldn't care less about the superficial world of media entertainment and placating high-maintenance stars and volatile executives. That had always been a bone of contention between them.

Christiane was the one better suited to running a studio. She loved the glamorous life and had married Leonard Green, one of TSW's executives. She enjoyed being the trophy wife and although she was at home raising two children, much of her time was spent hosting parties her husband threw.

Salim had always thought it a total waste that a studio like TSW would focus on lighthearted sitcoms and trashy talk shows. They should be making documentaries educating the public on the HIV situation in African countries, or life in war-torn Iraq.

He rapped on the door while Diane hissed behind him, "Salim, come on now. Your dad's in the middle of an interview."

Without waiting for an invitation, Salim waltzed in. He found the mogul on his knees in front of the seated woman he was supposedly interviewing. Tanner looked up, his pinched expression reflecting his surprise.

Salim cleared his throat. It was obvious what the dirty old goat had been up to or was about to do. And to think he'd admired the woman and thought she was classy.

Tanner slowly got to his feet, dusting the lint off his slacks.

"I gave Diane instructions I was not be disturbed," he said all bluster.

"Yes, I know."

The woman was watching them intently. She didn't seem overly concerned.

"Your pearl earring has to be here somewhere, Kennedy," Tanner said, brusquely. "I'll have the cleaners look for it before they vacuum. If it can't be found I'll replace it."

As though Salim was supposed to believe that. So much for initial impressions; wholesome she was not. She was just another ho, except this one was more cleaned up.

The studio head now stood with his arms crossed. He was a tall, distinguished-looking man with silvering hair, wide shoulders, a bit of a gut and an intimidating stance. Yet women were drawn to him like a magnet. Salim never could understand why. It certainly couldn't be his overbearing personality, so he had to attribute it to his power and wealth. And Tanner was a powerful man with influential contacts.

"When a door's closed it usually means a person is busy," his father barked.

"I knocked. You wanted to see me and here I am." Salim glanced at his watch. "I have to be some place in exactly thirty-five minutes."

His father's woman stood, smoothing the skirt that had slid up to her thighs. She was as cool and brassy as they came.

"Thank you for your time, Mr. Washington," she said. "You've certainly given me a lot to think about. May I get back to you tomorrow with an answer?"

She sounded formal, almost prim; a departure from the usual classless type Tanner went for. It was an act, had to be.

"Of course you may, and if I can do anything more to help make up your mind, don't hesitate to call." Tanner handed her a business card. "I'll see you out."

With a smile and a nod she made her way by Salim. Tanner stopped for a moment to make introductions.

"Kennedy Fitzgerald is a leadership consultant. I'm hopeful that she will soon join our team of executives. Kennedy, this is my son, Salim."

Kennedy's handshake was brief but firm. Salim swallowed the bile at the back of his throat. The audacity of the old man, hiring a woman he was involved with, as if he hadn't embarrassed his wife, Lucinda, enough.

"It's a pleasure to meet you. Were you in the lobby earlier?" Kennedy Fitzgerald asked.

"I was."

Salim took his time looking her over, letting his eyes slowly slide up and down her long legs. She wore sensible pumps and her navy suit reminded him of a banker. The plain white blouse under it covered her full breasts. Kennedy's hair was held back from her face with a tortoiseshell headband and was evenly trimmed.

Now he knew that conservative outfit was a cover. The sparkle in those slightly slanted eyes indicated she was not as prim as she looked. He'd seen with his own eyes his father on his knees between those long legs of hers.

"Is something wrong?" the Fitzgerald woman asked as he continued to stare.

"Actually, I was thinking that you might not be a very good fit for a television studio. Creative artsy types tend to get wild and you are as conservative as they come."

"Am I, now?"

She was as cool as an icicle. He doubted anything rattled her.

Tanner's brows furrowed and his eyes flashed disapprovingly. Salim continued to smile. Tanner nodded curtly in his direction. He held his latest by the elbow and eased her toward the door.

"We'll talk tomorrow. If I can do anything to sweeten the pot just let me know," he said, closing the door behind her.

Arms folded across his chest and gut, camouflaged in an expensive suit, Tanner faced Salim. "How dare you!"

"How dare I what?"

"You come barging in here when you obviously knew I was in a meeting."

"You said you wanted to see me. You had Diane call."

Salim looked directly into the eyes of the man he'd

been told he was the spitting image of. At thirty-three he refused to be intimidated. They looked nothing alike. He favored his mother, not this arrogant man with the overinflated ego.

"And you informed Diane you were too busy and couldn't make the time to meet with me. You said you were jet-lagged."

"I was. I still am."

"But you made the time to see your mother."

"I always have time for my mother."

Unlike you. The unspoken words hung between them.

"Have a seat," Tanner said, waving Salim toward a huge black leather couch.

The casting couch.

He'd be damned if he sat down on that thing. Who knew what disgusting things lived in that sofa?

"I prefer to stand," Salim answered, arms also folded, mimicking the man who had given him life. "What's so urgent that it required me being here? We haven't spoken in months."

"That was your decision," Tanner reminded him quietly.

Yes, indeed it had been his decision. He was sick and tired of watching this man hurt his mother. Their lifestyles were so very different anyway. Tanner loved living large and enjoyed the glitz and glamour that came with the television business. Salim despised it. He much preferred to do something useful like help change lives. His money was used to make a difference in other people's circumstances. That's why his last jaunt to Africa had been so satisfying. He'd enjoyed seeing what a little money could do to enhance lives. This upcoming trip would be even more rewarding. The clinic in Haiti badly needed staffing and money for medical supplies. He'd managed to get some substantial contributions.

A few years ago Salim and a partner had started a foundation that helped promote safe sex globally. Their ultimate goal was to educate and stem the transmittal of the HIV virus, particularly in some African and Caribbean countries.

The good thing about having a trust fund was that it gave him the freedom to travel and donate funds as he saw fit. A nine-to-five job would not allow him to pick up and leave whenever he wanted to. Of course he preferred not to remember that TSW Studios made his way of life possible.

"Perhaps you had better take a seat," Tanner repeated, his expression serious. "What I am going to say will take some time, and then we'll need to meet with the lawyers. There's some paperwork to go over."

Since it sounded serious Salim sat. He would strangle the old bastard with his bare hands if he told him he was going to divorce his mother and replace her with a younger model.

Kennedy Fitzgerald to be exact.

* * *

Kennedy had a lot to think about. Tanner Washington's job offer had come out of the blue, and at the perfect time. But it sounded as though she would be a glorified babysitter. Tanner wanted to hire her to groom his son, who appeared to be a handful. Kennedy was to get him ready to take over Tanner's position as studio head.

The television mogul had admitted to already having three heart attacks. He was now being scheduled for bypass surgery. His doctor had advised him to get his affairs in order, and this was where Kennedy came in. Tanner Washington was being forced to think of his mortality.

Kennedy still hadn't heard word one from Marna. Now Kennedy needed every penny she could get. First there was the matter of transportation to get her around. Her car could very easily be on its way to an auction block, which meant buying another. She'd already used a sizeable chunk of the money earned in Japan to get her bills current, and she dreaded thinking of how that delinquency would affect her credit.

She could kill the woman. Maybe Lincoln, her brother—named after Abraham Lincoln—knew of Marna's whereabouts. He still lived in eastern Washington where they'd grown up. Kennedy put in her earpiece and punched in the programmed number on her cell phone.

Lincoln's deep voice brought a smile to her face.

"Hey, baby girl. I bet you're glad to be home?"

"It was nice of you to call and check on me," Kennedy said sarcastically.

Linc's deep laughter rang out. "Don't get attitude with me. I'm a family man and plenty busy with the new baby. What's up?"

"Have you heard from Marna?"

"Was I supposed to? The last I knew she'd taken off to Alaska after some guy."

"What! She was supposed to be house-sitting for me."

"Yeah, I'd heard something about that. She's got this friend Betsy you might want to call."

After an extended hold Linc returned with Betsy's number. Hanging up, Kennedy called the number and became even more frustrated when she was kicked into voice mail. Having no choice, she left a message. Next on the agenda was the towing company.

"A silver Honda?" the stressed employee repeated while several phones rang in the background.

"Yes, yes," Kennedy said impatiently, giving her license plate number and mentally ticking off a dozen things she needed to do.

"Sorry, ma'am, but that vehicle is no longer here. When cars are repossessed they get wholesaled out to dealers. Yours could be on any number of trucks heading anywhere."

Seconds from losing it, Kennedy hung up the phone. She couldn't believe the mess her life had become.

Chapter 3

"**I**'ve decided to accept the position but on one condition," Kennedy said to Tanner Washington two days later.

"I'm delighted. What's the condition?"

"Your generous offer has to come with a company vehicle."

Tanner's rich laughter rang out. "All of my executives have company vehicles or at the very least they receive a car allowance."

Yes! Kennedy covered the phone's mouthpiece before she could say the word out loud. She exhaled the breath she didn't know she was holding. Things were definitely looking up.

After doing a little more digging, she'd learned her vehicle had been wholesaled out. Gone was the forty-eight hundred dollars she'd shelled out over the past year in car payments. The rental she was now driving was costing her a fortune, and to add insult to injury she hadn't been able to use a credit card, and that meant more money coming out of her bank account.

"There are several makes and models of cars you can choose from, but most of our executives drive a Lexus," Tanner added. "Come by and get the contract from my assistant, Diane. You'll need to sign it before you pick out a car."

"What's my start date?" Kennedy asked, already feeling a whole lot better. She took long, steadying breaths and waited for Tanner's response. She was just about to seal the most lucrative deal of her life that could very well help get her back on solid ground.

"I'd like you to start yesterday," Tanner Washington said. "My son, Salim, is going to be a challenge. He's headstrong and not really cooperative when told what to do. I had to enlist the help of his mother to help him see things my way."

"You mentioned you were having surgery. When is it planned for?"

"When you come in we'll talk about it. I've got a meeting in exactly two minutes. Let me transfer you to Diane."

He didn't wait for her to agree but simply handed her off to his assistant.

"This is Diane," a no-nonsense voice said into Kennedy's ear.

Kennedy tamped down on her excitement. She had a job and that meant income. Her credit had taken an enormous hit thanks to Marna's irresponsibility and in a short time her previously orderly world had turned into a nightmare. Bill collectors had been calling, and she'd had to go to the various utility companies to pay her water, gas and light bills before they were shut off.

Free yoga classes at her local community center were keeping her calm and she'd resumed her fast walking. The phone rang and Kennedy inhaled, anticipating another demanding creditor. It was not in her nature to dodge or use the answering machine to screen calls, but she was strongly considering that option.

"Hello?" she said.

Her mother's breathless voice came at her. "Honey, I was so worried about you. Why haven't you been answering your cell phone?"

Her mother Taiko Myers, had been on her honeymoon in Hawaii when Kennedy returned to the States. This latest marriage would be her fourth. Kennedy hoped she'd made a better choice this time around.

"I never got your message. I would have called you back. How was your honeymoon, Mom?" Kennedy prepared herself for the lengthy discussion that would surely follow.

Ten minutes later she managed to get in the first word. Kennedy used that opportunity to take the conversation in an entirely different direction.

"Have you heard from Marna, Mom?"

"Not recently. She's supposedly in Alaska with some guy she met in Seattle."

"She was supposed to be house-sitting for me and paying my bills with the rent she collected."

"Didn't she turn that job over to her friend Summer?"

Kennedy's right eye began to twitch. "Summer? I've never heard of a friend Summer."

"Taiko!" a gruff male voice called in the background.

"I'll be right there."

"Taiko. I need you. Where's my clean socks?"

Kennedy hadn't met stepfather number three, but from the sound of things, her mother had picked another winner. She tended to go for controlling, abusive types. Growing up, Kennedy had learned to insulate herself from the succession of men in and out of her mother's life. More than one had been far too interested in her.

The uncertainty of coming home and finding her mother in tears had made her wary and cynical of men in general. If this was what relationships were about, she wanted no part of them.

"Who's Summer?" Kennedy asked, focusing her mother back to the topic.

"Summer is Marna's best friend," Taiko explained. "I may have her number somewhere. If I find it, I'll call you back."

"Get your ass off the phone," her mother's latest screamed. "I need to get dressed."

Stepfather number three was shaping up to be just like the others.

"I've got to help Jack find something," her mother explained hurriedly.

"Call me back with Summer's number, Ma," Kennedy reminded her before hanging up.

"Okay, baby. I will."

Salim disconnected the call and clipped the phone back on his waistband. He cradled his head and groaned loudly. The airline had charged him a considerable penalty for canceling his ticket to Haiti. That one-hundred-dollar cancellation fee could have fed numerous orphans or treated HIV-positive babies. Wasting that money made him angry and thinking about what he would be responsible for in the next several months made him even angrier.

He was not at all interested in the television business, nor was he cut out to be an executive. But now he was expected to step into his father's shoes and make decisions that meant nothing to him. It seemed ironic that after doing everything he could to avoid the corporate trap, fate had dealt him this blow.

Much as he despised his father, it was his father's money that had allowed him to travel to third world, HIV-ridden countries. And no matter how much Salim disliked his dad, Tanner was sick and someone had to at least try and keep the company running. It was the whole family's livelihood. But that didn't mean he had to be happy about it.

The cell phone clipped to his waistband played a rhythmic jingle.

"It's Diane," his father's assistant said in her no-nonsense voice. "What's your schedule like for Thursday this week?"

"I was supposed to be in Haiti. Now it seems I am free."

"Good. I'm scheduling a meeting for 2:00 p.m. Please be sure to be on time."

"And the agenda is?" Salim probed.

"That I don't know, but the newly hired leadership consultant will be there, as well."

"Leadership consultant? Tell me you're kidding."

"Didn't you meet the young woman?"

"If I did, she wasn't very memorable."

"Her name is Kennedy Fitzgerald. She was being interviewed last week when you were here. That was the day you barged in on your father."

Salim recalled the woman in the blue business suit,

the one he'd thought classy and different, until he'd realized she was involved with his father.

"Uh, she's a leadership consultant?" he scoffed. "I've heard it called a lot of things."

"Actually she has excellent credentials, and as of this week she's officially on the payroll. I'm going to have to run, I have several phones ringing."

When Diane hung up, Salim paced for several minutes before making another call. Why would TSW Studios need a leadership consultant? Maybe they planned on shooting a sitcom about a life coach and the woman had agreed to be the consultant. More likely, his father needed a legitimate reason to keep his girlfriend around. What gumption and what a total waste of money. Money he could use to do something good.

He decided to call his sister, Christiane. She was usually good at putting things in perspective.

"Salim, it's good to hear from you," Christiane said the moment she heard his voice.

They caught up on the family issues before he broached his real reason for calling.

"Did you know that the old man had three minor heart attacks and is now scheduled for bypass surgery?" he asked.

"No I didn't!" Christiane cried. "Dad's never said a word, but that explains his frequent trips to Houston. They have some of the best heart surgeons there. Mom must have known something about this, but she never let on."

"That's because the old buzzard told her to keep her mouth shut. You know she'll do whatever he asks," Salim muttered bitterly.

"Oh, Salim, there you go again. Can't you make peace with Dad and move on? He could probably use your help and support right now."

Salim snorted. "In that case he shouldn't have hired his girlfriend to work at the studio."

"What!"

"You heard me. I know squat about the television business and now I'm being railroaded into coming on board." A horrifying thought gripped him, one he was reluctant to put into words.

"You have no proof," Christiane admonished. "Dad's pushing sixty. He's getting up there in years and we're the only two children he has. Why is it you always want to believe the worst of him?"

"I can't summon up compassion for a liar and a cheat. Don't you recall what he put our mother through growing up?"

"You and your assumptions."

"Not assumptions. There's been proof." Salim began to recite events and situations, all captured either on film or in the newspaper.

But there was no swaying Christiane to his way of thinking. She was Daddy's girl, always was and always would be.

Perhaps it was high time he paid a visit home.

Talking to his mother on the phone was one thing, but seeing her face-to-face was another. He'd planned on taking her out to lunch and giving her the gift he'd brought back from Africa anyway. There was no danger of running into the old man midafternoon, so why not just go on over?

Rather than take his pickup truck, he opted for his Vespa scooter. There was something about riding that sleek machine with the wind blowing in his face and the motor throbbing between his legs that made him feel invincible. He'd always marched to the beat of his own drummer anyway, and he wasn't about to change.

Zooming in and out of traffic, Salim whipped across the bridge and onto Mercer Island where the family had its home. He navigated several winding roads before heading up a tree-lined driveway. He left the Vespa parked in front of the rambling brick mansion that he'd called home growing up.

Salim used the house key he kept on his key ring, but seldom used.

"Salim. Did somebody die?" Tilly the housekeeper who'd been a second mother to him asked as he sailed through the front door. She wiped her hands on the apron wrapped around her ample waist.

"No, no one died. I'm here to see my mother and you." He gave her the full force of his smile.

"Consider yourself lucky that I like you," she said, offering up a plump cheek for his kiss. Matilda, Tilly for short, was one of those rotund, ageless women whose fat prevented her from wrinkling.

She frowned at him. "You need to leave those muddy boots on the doormat. The floors were just done and I'll be damned if I'm going to have you mess them up. How was Africa or wherever you're coming from this time?"

"Lots of work, Tilly. I'm exhausted." Salim slipped off his boots and left them where she'd instructed.

"Your mother's in the bedroom. She has one of her headaches, probably brought on by you," Tilly snorted. "Is that gift for her?"

"Yes, it is."

Salim left her and headed down a long hallway toward his mother's bedroom. Although she didn't think he knew it, it had been years since she and Tanner had shared a room. The old man's room was on the opposite end of the hall close to the staircase so that he could come and go as he pleased.

What a way to live.

Salim knocked lightly. He heard a stirring from inside and then his mother's voice came at him.

"Tilly, didn't I say I didn't want to be disturbed?"

"It's me, Mother."

"Salim! You're back." There was genuine joy in her tone. "What brings you here? I would've thought you'd be home sleeping and jet-lagged."

The door opened slowly. Lucinda, dressed in an

elegant silk robe, embraced him. It reminded him of when he was a little boy and got hurt. It was always his mother's arms he sought.

They'd always had a special bond. Lucinda understood his need to carve out a life for himself. Her easygoing nature and acceptance of others made her a pushover for her dominant husband. It made Salim want to protect her. And protect her he did.

"I came to see my favorite woman," Salim answered when he was able to separate himself from her lily scent. The smell of lilies was one of his first memories. To this day just a whiff took him back in time to a place when life was so much simpler.

Lucinda whacked his arm. "I bet that's what you say to all your girls. If you'll give me a few minutes to change, I'll have Tilly fix us something to eat."

Salim handed her the gift he'd brought all the way back from Zimbabwe. In exchange he received another tight hug.

"Oh, Salim, you shouldn't have, but I'm glad you did. This jewelry box is beautiful. Give me five minutes to get dressed and then meet me in the sunroom."

True to her word, Lucinda arrived in the sunroom at the appointed time. Salim was already comfortably seated in a wingback chair, sipping bottled water and watching a muted television with one eye. When he stood, she wrapped him in another tight embrace.

"What's really brought you here?" she asked,

holding Salim away from her and examining him with a critical eye.

"I came to talk to you," he answered.

"About?"

"What's going on with your husband's health?"

"Did your father say something to you?" his mother hedged.

"The old man summoned me to the studio, Mom. He says he has health issues. It's the first time I've heard of heart problems. If I'm being manipulated I'd like to know. I canceled a ticket to Haiti and put my life on hold. Tell me what's going on."

"He didn't want you or Christiane to worry," Lucinda said in a soft voice.

"Really? All his life it's always been about him."

Lucinda took the chair across from Salim and crossed a shapely leg. Salim sat back down and waited for his mother to begin.

"Your father is not the ogre you make him out to be. If he's reaching out to you, it's because he needs you to step up and take over. The diagnosis from his doctor is not good."

Salim cracked his knuckles so hard Lucinda flinched.

He didn't know what to say. "Why didn't you call me and warn me this was coming, Ma? I'm not management material. I don't even own a suit."

She held up a hand, silencing him. "A suit does not

make the man. You'll have plenty of help running TSW. Your dad pays his executive team well for their expertise. What we need is a strong presence at the studio while I nurse him back to health."

The comment propelled Salim out of his seat. He snorted and began circling the room. "The whole corporate thing makes me want to gag, Ma. I'm not much for the politics or phony people."

"Then let's not talk about the situation," Lucinda said, accepting the cup of tea Tilly handed her. "Tell me about Africa. The jewelry box you brought me is quite lovely and very well crafted. I'll use it to keep my everyday rings."

For the next hour while they visited, Lucinda caught him up on what was happening in her life and he shared his. She shared how worried she was about Tanner's upcoming surgery.

Despite Salim's feelings about his father, he threaded his fingers through his mother's and squeezed her hand hard. Lucinda sniffled loudly and took a sip from her cup. Speaking more to herself than to him, she said, "There's nothing more relaxing than a well-brewed cup of tea."

By subtly shifting the conversation, they ended the visit on an upbeat note.

In an overt act of rebelliousness, Salim arrived at TSW studios on Thursday in jeans and a long-sleeved shirt that had seen better days. His father was nowhere to be found when he arrived. Diane made the usual excuses.

"Your dad's in a meeting," she said, pointing him to a seat and picking up yet another phone. Salim soon got tired of hanging out in the waiting area. He was about to take a walk when along came Kennedy Fitzgerald. Today she was dressed in another of those sharp conservative suits.

Today's getup was a pin-striped suit, the skirt skimming the knees of her beautifully shaped legs. Pearls circled her neck and she sported matching earrings. No one dressed like this in Seattle, not even the lawyers. But Kennedy Fitzgerald made her conservative suit look becoming, even sexy.

The three-inch heels of her pumps beat out a *rat-a-tat* as she approached Diane's desk.

"I'm a few minutes early," she said in a very refined voice.

"Unfortunately, Mr. Washington is running a few minutes late. Why don't you introduce yourself to Salim, his son? He's seated over there." Di pointed a finger to the corner where he was seated. "You two are in the same meeting and this may be a good opportunity to get acquainted."

He could kill Diane. She'd put him in a spot. Now he couldn't very well walk away without being rude. He forced himself to smile, wave and pat the spot next to him. "Please join me. There's plenty of space."

Kennedy looked at him as if she smelled something slightly unpleasant. She started toward him gingerly.

The words popped out of his mouth before he could stop them.

"You look lovely," he said.

He was surprised when Kennedy Fitzgerald actually had the grace to blush.

Chapter 4

Kennedy picked up on the tension between father and son. Salim remained slouched in a chair, not saying a word, while his father outlined his plan. Thunderous was the only way to describe his expression. He made no secret he was not at all happy about what his father was planning.

"When are you expecting to step down from your position?" Kennedy asked the studio head.

"My surgery is scheduled for two weeks from today. I'll be here to at least transition Salim into his role."

"And what are you expecting me to accomplish during those two weeks?" Kennedy asked, jotting notes as the senior Washington spoke.

"First things first. Salim will have to learn to dress the part of a successful executive."

"Are you expecting her to take me shopping?" Salim sneered, at last breaking his silence.

"No, there's no time. We'll have a tailor and a personal shopper come onto the premises. Kennedy can help you pick out your suits, shirts and ties."

Salim glared at Kennedy. "The hell she will!"

When she'd accepted the job of grooming Salim Washington into the man his father thought he could be, she knew it would be no easy task. From the very beginning she'd seen *rebel* written all over him, but at the same time there was a restless, adventuresome spirit that she'd found very attractive.

"You're stepping into the role of president of a prestigious television studio," his father reminded him quietly. "You need to look the part."

"That may be so but I don't require a woman to dress me, nor do I need another mother."

"Kennedy is a leadership consultant."

"And a total waste of company money."

Salim popped out of his seat and bounded toward the window. He turned his back on both of them and stared out onto the parking lot.

The conversation continued as if he didn't exist. Ignoring his son, Tanner Washington handed Kennedy a sheet of paper.

"I've highlighted and prioritized everything I expect you to accomplish."

Kennedy glanced at the paper because that was what was expected of her.

"I'm expected to teach your son table manners?" she asked in a low voice.

"I'm expecting that you'll teach him how to be a gracious host. Now, if that includes knowing which fork to use, and when to use it, then so be it. This position requires he entertain influential people."

"Don't talk about me as if I don't exist," Salim groused. "How long will I have to put up with Ms. Fitzgerald shadowing me?"

Tanner took his son's ill humor in stride. "For as long as it takes. The sooner you get your hands around this business and work on your people skills, the sooner you'll be on your own. I don't anticipate being out very long. People with heart transplants are on their feet in days, and this is bypass surgery."

Kennedy privately thought the older Washington man was being overly optimistic.

Salim's glance took in his father's spacious surroundings. The suite was larger than most people's apartments and had several rooms.

"Will Ms. Fitzgerald have her own space or are you expecting me to share this office with her?" he barked.

"I haven't decided yet."

"I won't share an office. I refuse to be babysat."

"We'll see," his father responded in the same level tone he'd had from the beginning of their meeting.

Salim returned to stand in front of his father's desk. He held out his hand for a copy of the paper that Kennedy was reading.

"If you're going to set expectations, then you might as well share them with me," he snapped.

"I'll have Diane print you up another copy."

In an attempt to defuse what she saw as a conflict in the making, Kennedy handed her paper to Salim.

He held it gingerly between his fingers and scanned it quickly. "You gotta be kidding! You're expecting me to be joined to this woman's hip. She's to teach me how to small-talk and stay away from controversial topics. The only thing she's not to do is diaper me. Forget about it!"

A sarcastic laugh followed. Salim slapped down the list, made an abrupt turn and headed for the door.

"A substantial donation to AIDS research is at risk here," his father shouted after him. "I'll stop contributing to your trust fund if that's what it takes. Just think about all those poor people in Haiti that you currently support."

"You really are unconscionable," Salim gritted out, sending his father a fiery look before he disappeared.

"It's a big change for your son," Kennedy said after Salim had left. She'd always played the role of peacemaker on the job. "He just might need a little time to digest everything you've said. You've hit him with quite a bit and he's probably having difficulty coping with your health issues. Children often think of parents as invincible."

Privately she thought it was an awful thing to do, blackmailing your own child. At the same time she was curious about the Haiti reference. Prickly as Salim was, she had the feeling there was a caring man somewhere deep inside. She had to give him credit for standing up to an intimidating man and being true to himself.

"My son's always been a challenging personality," Tanner said, rising and coming to sit across from her. "He could give two hoots about money. He uses it only to benefit someone else. Shall we get the other items on our agenda nailed down? Diane will arrange for you to tour the studio afterward."

For the next half hour the studio head talked about his expectations, and what he hoped Kennedy would accomplish with his son.

"I'm tossing in a bonus," Tanner added as they wound down their business. "You whip Salim into shape and you can have your own television program. Take your life coaching to the masses."

Kennedy's excitement began to build. What he was proposing was better than immediate cash in her pocket. She could be a household name like her idol, Oprah.

"That's an interesting proposal but I'm not sure anyone would be interested in me," she said.

"Don't sell yourself short. With a bit of marketing and the right exposure you could be one of TSW's rising stars."

Kennedy tamped down on her excitement. She'd accepted the position because of money and the company car that came with it; a television show was a very nice offer but she couldn't afford to get carried away.

Even so, her heart was palpitating so fast she thought she might have an attack. A television show meant exposure and more clients than she needed. All that translated into cold, hard cash. Plus, she really enjoyed what she did so this could take her career to a whole new level.

"Here's what I'm thinking," Tanner Washington said. "We make it a reality show where select members of the audience share issues they are having. They're paired off and sent to a place similar to the Dr. Phil house, just like you see on his show. Three months later we bring them back. Now the studio audience gets to vote as to who's made the most progress. The program would be cutting edge. Ratings are bound to soar. And I can see you'd be very telegenic."

"It would certainly be different from the usual line-up," Kennedy said diplomatically. "Can you give me some time to mull this over?" she asked, not wanting to appear too anxious. "I'm not sure I'm cut out for show business."

In the back of her mind she thought this was a no-brainer, but it was smart not to sound too eager.

Tanner rebutted with "What's there to think about? Most people would be champing at the bit given this opportunity."

"I'm not most people."

Tanner chuckled as if he thought her answer was the funniest thing he'd heard. "That's exactly why I hired you. You've got credentials most people only dream of. What's impressed me is that a young black woman had the foresight to learn Japanese and French along with her native English."

"Thank you. My grandmother is Japanese and I learned to speak the language at an early age. French I studied in school and spent a year abroad perfecting." Kennedy glanced at her watch. "If we're done I'm going to have to run. I have a dinner appointment."

"No time for a tour, then?" Tanner asked, walking her to the door and handing her over to Diane.

"I can do a quick one."

"Diane will get you all set up."

"Happy to," Tanner's assistant said, taking over.

Kennedy scanned the general area realizing for the first time that Salim was sprawled in one of the chairs. He was waiting, she presumed, to speak to his father. She would not be a witness to that confrontation.

"Did I hear something about Ms. Fitzgerald needing a tour?" he asked, deigning to get up.

"Yes, your dad asked me to find someone to show her around."

"You just did. I'll take over from here, Diane," Salim said, smiling at his father's assistant.

Kennedy's gut told her she was in for a treat. It was the first time she'd seen what looked like a genuine smile light up Salim's rugged features, and again she was struck by what a difference that made. He was the kind of man who looked as if he stepped off a Field and Stream cover.

She glanced pointedly at the clock on the far wall. "I'm sorry but we'll need to make this quick. I have to be some place in about forty-five minutes."

"Ten minutes will take care of things. I'll give you a quick walk-through and point out the highlights."

It surprised Kennedy that he was even offering. She really couldn't quite believe it. He'd made his dislike of her so apparent. There had to be something in it for him.

Salim held on to Kennedy's upper arm, guiding her down another long carpeted hallway. She felt an inner tremor and dismissed it as a delayed reaction to her interview. As they walked, he pointed out the celebrities whose pictures adorned the walls.

"Hey, Salim," an attractive man who looked vaguely familiar said as he swung by them.

"David McFarland," Salim supplied. "And in case you haven't kept up, he's a popular soap actor."

Kennedy wasn't a big fan of soaps, but she did recall seeing the man on a couple of talk shows and she remembered hearing something about David being the current flavor of the month.

They toured a construction area where sets were being built and Salim pointed out the warehouses where props were stored. Kennedy got to see the set where a popular talk show was filmed. On another set, a special effects machine created a winter storm. When they came to white double doors, Salim slowed down.

"This is our commissary. We can get something to drink if you'd like," he said.

And even though Kennedy had promised her other brother, Roosevelt, that she'd meet him at his place in Edmonds for dinner, she was curious about this man with his mercurial changes of mood.

"I can if we make it quick."

Salim left her seated in a comfortable booth and went off to get their drinks. He had a loose-limbed walk to him and the view from the rear set off a number of erotic fantasies.

While she waited for him to get back, Kennedy looked at the activity around her. The couple in a nearby booth were fighting, and from the looks of things the woman was winning hands down. The table across from Kennedy held several burly types who looked as though they worked construction. Their casual, dusty clothing was a sure giveaway, and she guessed they were grips, the people who moved scenery.

"This is a busy place," Kennedy's escort said, sliding into the seat across from her and shoving a foam cup her way.

"I can tell. Is there something you wanted to say to me?"

"Yes, as a matter of fact there is. I've never wanted anything to do with this studio. The money from my trust fund is at stake, and my mother's pleadings and her livelihood are the only reason I'm here."

"Surprise, surprise."

A pair of light brown eyes bored into hers. She could sense the internal anger and wondered what she'd done to deserve such animosity. There was definitely something else underlying Salim's barely concealed resentment.

"I am very protective of my mother," he warned. "And I will do just about anything to ensure that she doesn't get hurt."

"As you should be. And you think I'll hurt your mother how?"

"You tell me. Let's not play games. My father is an ill man. I want my mother to be taken care of in the manner to which she is accustomed. And I'll fight you tooth and nail if you make an attempt to lay claim to a dime of my father's estate."

Kennedy took a deep, calming breath.

"You'd stand to gain quite a bit yourself," she countered. "This conversation is highly insulting."

Those light-colored eyes flickered over her again. They issued a direct challenge.

"The important thing is we understand each other."

"What exactly are you interested in?" she asked, curious to see what made him tick.

Another hard stare was directed her way.

"I'm interested in children dying of malnutrition because there's not enough food to go around. My heart aches for women in poor countries contracting AIDS because of irresponsible, selfish partners. Every time I read about orphaned children scratching themselves to sleep for lack of human touch, my stomach churns. All that aside, I don't want my mother hurt, not the way she's been hurt her entire life."

"Why would I want to hurt your mother?" Kennedy asked carefully.

"Some women think taking a married man away from his wife is proof that they still have it."

The conversation was over with as far as she was concerned. "You think I'm having an affair with your father?"

"This position, Leadership Consultant, was created especially for you. He's paying you a small fortune to come on board. Why would he do that unless he was sleeping with you?"

Kennedy just stared at him, then slid from the booth.

Nothing she said or did would change his impression of her anyway.

"For the record, I am always professional and am not having an affair with your dad. It's insulting you would think so. I have to go. This has been a most enlightening conversation," she said.

"Enlightening for me, as well," Salim answered, falling in step with her.

In the lobby she handed the security guard her pass and stuck her hand out. "Thanks for the tour. It'll be interesting to work with you."

He let her hand dangle. After a beat or two she shoved it into her suit jacket pocket. Enough was enough.

"I'll be watching your every move," he said in the same icy voice.

"I'm being paid to watch yours. We don't have to like each other, just work together."

Kennedy pushed through the revolving doors. What an obnoxious man he was. So that's what he wanted. To warn me.

It would take a lot more than a recalcitrant spoiled, rich kid to ruffle her feathers. Her number-one goal was getting her own life back in order. And this job was certainly going to help.

Chapter 5

That night Salim nursed his beer while watching the ferries go in and out of the harbor. He'd always found the whole process of embarkation and debarkation fascinating. His best friend and partner, Nate, slouched on the bar stool to his right. He was pretending to sip his drink when in reality he was checking out the woman across from him. Salim looked at Nate and chuckled.

"What's so amusing?" Nate asked

"I was just thinking about you and me getting into trouble."

"I've never gotten you into trouble. I still can't believe you're seriously considering working at your father's studio. Didn't you once tell me there wasn't a prayer in hell?"

Salim's bitter laughter rang out. "I don't have much choice. The old man's having surgery and I'm doing it for my mother, not him."

"Do you even own a suit?" Nate snickered.

"I bought one for my sister's wedding."

"Does it still fit?"

Salim took a long pull on his beer and ignored him, but Nate persisted.

"What's this about your father hiring someone to whip you into shape?"

"She's called Kennedy Fitzgerald and her title is Leadership Consultant. The old man had to come up with some reason for her being hired."

"That's one hot babe across from us," Nate said, changing the subject. "Do you think I still have what it takes?"

Salim glanced in the direction his friend was looking. "Hard to say."

"Man, you're really good for my ego."

The waterfront establishment where they'd gone to grab a drink wasn't fancy. The clientele was your average Joe.

"Should I?" Nate asked, an eye to the oblivious woman.

"You have nothing to lose," Salim answered, taking another pull on his beer. "Don't let me hold you up."

Nate raised his beer bottle, saluting the woman. When she acknowledged him with a nod, he was off the stool and heading over.

Salim's thoughts returned to the attractive woman his old man had hired to turn him into a corporate stiff. Anger bubbled up inside him. He had been on his way to Haiti to complete a project that was already behind. This unexpected turn of events would ruin everything.

Not that he was totally selfish; if the old man did have serious medical problems, then yes, it was his duty to step up and do what he could. But a television studio was the last thing he wanted to run. Plus, while he didn't like his dad, he certainly didn't want him six feet under.

Salim's trust fund had made life much easier for him and the people who depended on his largesse. It had allowed him to set up a foundation helping those in Third World countries less fortunate than he.

The foundation was funded by donations from major corporations and several independent benefactors. He'd planned to leave for Haiti in the next few days, where he and Nate were building a clinic run by medical volunteers.

When Salim's cell phone rang he glanced at the number and frowned. What did his sister, Christiane, want? They'd spoken the evening before.

"Hey," Salim said. "What's up?"

"Has Mother called you?" Christiane asked, sounding as though she was choking.

"Not that I know of. I haven't checked my messages. Is something wrong?"

"You haven't heard?"

"Uh-uh."

Salim caught Nate's eye. He was making progress with the jeans-clad woman across the way. They had their arms around each other and she was whispering in his ear. Nate winked.

"Dad was just rushed to the hospital," Christiane said, crying softly. "He had another attack. Mother is hysterical. She needs you."

Salim's breath caught. "Give me the name of the hospital and I'm on my way."

The words were barely out of Christiane's mouth before Salim hopped off the bar stool and motioned to Nate he was leaving. His friend's eyebrows rose and Salim signaled back he'd phone him later.

Although there was no love lost between Salim and the man who claimed to be his father, this didn't sound good.

His mother was his everything. He didn't plan on letting her or their family down.

"Ms. Fitzgerald, I'm going to need you to come in tomorrow. You'll be compensated, of course," Diane said the moment Kennedy picked up the phone.

Kennedy didn't like the way the assistant's voice warbled. Diane had a calm demeanor, as she recalled. *Something must have her shook.*

"Is everything okay?" she asked.

"No. Mr. Washington was rushed to the hospital. He had a heart attack. It's going to be some time before he's in any condition to resume his responsibilities. Salim will be filling in for him until he recovers."

"I'm so sorry. You can count on me being there."

Kennedy had been looking forward to using the next few days to get her life back in order. She'd used the money she'd made in Japan to pay off most of her credit card bills, and she'd contacted other creditors to see just how far behind she was. Within a short space of time she'd laid out an incredible amount of money. There went her savings.

Ed had come by, giving Kennedy the mailbox address he'd been sending his rental payments to. She'd immediately sent a note to the address, so hopefully she'd get a response soon. She'd also gotten the address of Marna's friend, Summer, and was planning to drive to Bothell tomorrow to see if she could talk to the woman.

"Can you come in at 7:00 a.m. tomorrow?" Diane asked. "We start early in the TV business."

"Sure."

Kennedy hung up thinking about what a strange turn her life had taken. She'd just seen Tanner at his most robust and bursting with energy. It was hard to picture him immobile in a hospital.

She put the vision of Tanner Washington out of her

mind and focused on more pleasant things. Her
brother Roosevelt and his girlfriend, Tamika, had
invited her to dinner. Lincoln, her other brother, and
his wife and baby were on their way in from eastern
Washington. It would be good to see the family. It had
been a while.

She floored the accelerator, making the trip from
Bellevue to Edmonds in less than thirty minutes. The
charming little town with its quaint downtown area and
houses on the edges of cliffs had always enchanted her.
Roosevelt and Tami, a glass blower, rented a small
cottage with a wonderful water view.

Lucy, a frisky golden retriever, greeted Kennedy the
minute she stepped out of the rented Focus.

"Hey, Luce," Kennedy said, scratching the dog
behind the ear. "Where are your owners?"

"The front door's unlocked," Tami called through an
open window.

"Lincoln's running late. He's stuck in rush-hour
traffic," Roosevelt added, linking an arm through hers
and hustling her into the kitchen, where Tami was pre-
siding over a pot far bigger than she.

Tami broke away to hug Kennedy. "You look tired.
Have you been getting sleep?"

Kennedy sighed. "Unfortunately, I'm still on
Tokyo time."

"Maybe this will help," Roosevelt said, pouring them
all glasses of wine.

He flopped into a kitchen chair and pulled out the chair next to him so Kennedy could sit down. "Tell me about this new job of yours."

Kennedy filled them in, telling them about Tanner Washington's medical condition. She was cut off by Lucy's excited barking.

"Linc's here," Roosevelt said, shooting up from his chair. "He'll need a hand with his suitcases and baby. Shelli probably has her hands full with all the side dishes."

For the next three hours there was a lot of eating, catching up and chasing the crawling baby. Shelli had brought along several dishes she claimed to have "just whipped up." She always put Kennedy and her nonexistent culinary talent to shame.

"Dinner is at my house the next time around. I'll make all the food," Kennedy promised. Now, they all knew that would never happen.

Kennedy told them about Tanner Washington's offer of her own show.

"That's way too cool," Shelli said, wiping the baby's nose at the same time.

"Just remember you've got a brother in the biz," Roosevelt added.

He was currently trying his hand at writing screenplays. The comment, although said half jokingly, had an underlying seriousness to it.

"You know you'd be the first person I brought on board."

"Can we talk about something else?" Tami inter-jected, amazingly in tune. "I'm sure Kennedy will do what she can to get you aboard. Let's talk about the upcoming family reunion."

"What reunion?" Kennedy asked, the thought of getting together with the blended family making her break out in hives for a number of reasons. Her memories of growing up were bittersweet.

"If we're going to have this gathering, we might as well get organized," Shelli said, finding a pad and paper in her purse.

"I'll plan the menu and arrange the catering," Tami volunteered.

"We're doing potluck again?" Shelli asked.

"Yes, but we still need to coordinate so that not everyone brings the same thing. I'll create the menu and assign each person a dish," Tami said.

Kennedy remained silent. *With all that this family has been through, we give new meaning to the phrase "family drama."* She'd learned to hold her own with the best of them and give as good as she got.

After growing up the way she did, reining in Salim Washington should be a cake walk.

Chapter 6

There was something about being seated behind the old man's desk that gave Salim immense satisfaction. In an overt act of rebellion, he'd shown up this morning in ripped jeans, T-shirt and sneakers. Although it was his first day filling in as president of TSW, he planned on being true to himself. No monkey suit for him.

Salim glanced down at his trusty Timex. He'd been there one whole hour and his handler still hadn't shown up; some coach she was turning out to be.

"Hey, Di," he called out to the reception area, hearing his father's assistant tip-tapping on her keyboard. Usually she rose with the chickens and was in before the first streak of dawn hit the sky. Today, however, he'd beaten her to it. Taking his legs off his father's glass desk and smirking with satisfaction at the smudges he'd left behind, he walked into the outer room where Diane sat. "Didn't you tell me that you called Ms. Fitzgerald to advise her our day began at seven? How come she's not here?"

"I did call Kennedy. She still has a couple of minutes before she is officially late."

"I'd think that on your first day on the job you'd be here with plenty of time to spare," Salim groused.

"Kennedy's coming in from Bellevue, there's always traffic on the bridge," Diane said calmly.

At ten after the hour when Kennedy still wasn't there, Salim again called to Diane.

"Does my leadership coach have a number? Being late the first day on the job doesn't bode well for us. I'm going to the commissary for coffee if she's not here in the next few minutes."

Normally patient, Diane smothered a groan. "I have Kennedy's phone number. Would you like me to do the honors or would you prefer to call yourself?"

"I'll do it," Salim said.

Just then Kennedy came rushing in.

"I'm sorry I'm late," she huffed. "There was an accident on the bridge and then I couldn't find parking."

"Excuses, excuses. I would have thought you would

have used your executive parking card to get into the other lot," Salim said coldly.

"I guess someone forgot to send me one," Kennedy lobbed back.

"I'll take care of it immediately," Diane said smoothly. "I overnighted a package with items such as your corporate credit card, parking card, et cetera. I'll check with the carrier and see if there's been a problem with delivery. Coffee?" she asked, smiling cheerfully.

"No need for you to put yourself out," Salim interjected. "Kennedy and I will walk to the commissary and get ourselves breakfast. Please show Kennedy to her office and she can meet me back here in ten minutes."

"Uh," Diane said, "didn't your father tell you that he expected you to share an office?"

Salim felt a stabbing pain at his temples. This was just not happening. He was not sharing an office with that woman. No way and no how. "Diane, we're going to breakfast and when I get back, I expect Kennedy will have her own office. I don't care whether you have to clear out a closet to make space, just find her something."

Kennedy was wise enough not to utter an objection.

"We'll need to make breakfast quick," she said, glancing at her BlackBerry. "In exactly forty-five minutes a personal shopper from Nordstrom's will be here with a tailor to fit you for suits. I asked him to bring along designer suits, shirts and ties. So we have half an hour to eat. At eleven o'clock we have a meeting with the executive staff, and then later there's a town hall meeting with all the employees."

"When did you plan all this?" Salim snapped.

"Diane helped. She and I coordinated and we scheduled the important meetings immediately. They're on your calendar and I sent you several e-mail reminders," Kennedy pointed out.

Diane jerked her thumb at an overflowing in-box and a neatly stacked pile on his desk, "Those are all your, uh, e-mails. I arranged them in order of importance. I also printed out your calendar." She turned her attention back to the computer monitor and began typing.

"Do you still want to go to the commissary or do you need time to plan your day?" Kennedy asked.

Salim slanted a look designed to make the strongest heart murmur. Despite the fact the woman irked him, dressed in the conservative pin-striped pantsuit, she was still hot. He shook his head, dismissing the picture of her stark naked. Refusing to get too carried away, he quickly pulled himself together.

"Diane, what else is on my calendar that I need to know about?" he asked.

"It's all printed out for you," she reminded him.

He grabbed the first piece of paper on the top of the pile, and kept walking with Kennedy following right behind.

On their way to the commissary several people flagged him down.

"How's your dad?" Mark, his godfather, a man with iron-gray hair and a slightly rumpled appearance, asked.

"Holding his own. He's still in intensive care but he's stable. Mother called and told me this morning."

"I'm glad to hear that. His are some mighty big shoes to fill. If you need anything, don't hesitate to call on me. I was your father's confidant and I have a good inkling of how his mind works."

Salim wasn't so sure anyone knew how the old man's mind worked. Salim introduced the executive to Kennedy.

"This is Mark Wallingford, TSW's vice president of Program Development, and also my godfather," he said. "Kennedy's a new hire and an expert at teaching leadership skills."

Mark nodded and smiled vaguely in Kennedy's direction. "Welcome! I didn't know we needed someone to train us on how to manage our people."

"Neither did I, but my old man seems to think we do."

Mark graciously allowed the comment to pass.

"I've been asked to come aboard and help Salim transition into the role of president," Kennedy said.

Mark looked as if he'd swallowed a golf ball. Shooting another vague smile Kennedy's way, he turned his attention back to Salim. "I'll get myself on your calendar and we'll go over some outstanding issues when you can fit me in."

"Salim!" a slim, dark-skinned young woman with dimples and hair held off her face by a flowing scarf exclaimed as she threw her arms around him.

"Charissa," Salim greeted, giving the woman a tight hug and almost lifting her off her feet. "I heard your sitcom's doing really well. You continue to get out-standing ratings."

"Does that mean I can demand a huge raise?" she asked cheekily. "I heard you were the acting president, so you can make it happen. How is your dad?"

"Stable and holding his own. If you come to the town hall meeting later, I'll fill you in."

"I'm there," she said with a toss of her flowing mane and scarf.

Charissa was the new "it" girl in town, adored and stalked by the paparazzi. For the last few months her face had been plastered on billboards nationally. She'd been the topic of the major tabloids: Everything from her taking up with aliens to getting married to the likes of Shemar Moore, another popular television actor.

She'd been linked to one bad boy after another, probably because she was well known for living on the edge. She and Salim had dated a couple of times but then both had rethought the involvement and decided they were better off as friends. Charissa was definitely high maintenance and Salim couldn't imagine her taking off for Senegal on a whim.

Remembering his manners, Salim prodded Kennedy

forward. "This is Kennedy Fitzgerald. She's our newly hired leadership coach."

"That's some fancy title," Charissa said, eyeing Kennedy curiously. "Good luck to you. Sorry but I have to run, I'm already late for filming."

The flowing scarf trailing behind her, she raced down the hallway, leaving them both breathless from all that energy.

"What a beautiful and unusual woman," Kennedy said, staring after her.

"Yes, Chari is quite unforgettable, and she knows it, too."

After running into several more people, all of whom stopped to inquire about his father, they finally made it into the commissary.

"We're going to have to eat quickly," Kennedy said once they were seated at a table toward the back of the room.

"First, you and I need to get a couple of things straight," Salim said, biting into a bagel.

"Yes?"

"I don't need babysitting. I'm here because of my obligations. I can't afford for my father to cut me off financially. And someone from the family needs to be at the helm of this company. We need to make sure our family is taken care of."

"Okay, now that I have that straight, what else?"

The Kennedy woman didn't seem to get bent out

of shape no matter what he said or did. She was one tough cookie.

"Second, I don't need a handler."

Kennedy set down the paper cup she'd been sipping from and met his stare. "I'm not looking forward to babysitting you, either. I've been hired to do a job and all I am asking is that you work with me."

Salim's light-colored eyes flickered over her chiseled features. Damn, she was gorgeous and playing the part of a professional to perfection, pretending that she really was an experienced leadership guru when they both knew this was a cover.

"Look," he said, "the old man needed an excuse to have you around. He created this position for you. If you stay out of my way I'll stay out of yours, and you and I will get along just fine."

When her eyebrows shot up slightly and she leaned in even closer, Salim thought she was even better looking than his initial impression. There was a simmering sensuality underlying the outwardly conservative appearance.

"Why would your father need an excuse to have me around?" she said in an even voice.

"Because it's obvious the two of you are having an affair. He's had no problem in the past flaunting his women. Maybe he's just become more discreet in his old age."

"You're mistaken," Kennedy snapped. "Your father

and I have no relationship other than employer and employee.

"Tell that to someone else. I know what I saw."

"What exactly did you see?" she challenged.

"Oh, come on. The day you were supposedly interviewed, the old man was on his knees. When I walked in you and he were about to be engaged in an intimate act, or you all had just finished."

Kennedy's eyes flashed fire, but she still maintained her composure. Standing, she said in even tones, "You've just crossed the line. How dare you assume such a thing? Your father was helping me to find a pearl earring. This conversation has just ended as far as I'm concerned. We need to get back."

Salim thought about what he saw. Perhaps she was telling the truth…perhaps. "You need to get back. I don't," he said, also standing. "If you're that good at what you do, then you pick out my clothing."

He wasn't some twelve-year-old kid whose mother was taking him to the store to try on his first suit.

"Fine," Kennedy said, shrugging. "It's entirely your option whether you choose to be present and have a say in what you'll be wearing for the next several months. All that's required is to show up for your eleven o'clock meeting, but make sure you're professionally dressed. You're the one who has to face the crowd and tell them you're assuming the role of TSW's president."

Kennedy's heels made a tip-tapping sound on the

wooden floor as she strode from the room. Salim soon caught up with her.

"Don't you ever walk away from me again," he gritted out, holding his hand on her wrist.

"Then act like an adult. You've admitted you know nothing about running a television studio. Why give the executive team more to talk about by showing up for that meeting like you've run away from home?"

God, she smelled good, too good to resist. He couldn't help it. He pulled her toward him and bent over to steal a kiss, a kiss that was met with resistance.

"Relax, sweetie. No need to get uptight."

"What is wrong with you?" Kennedy said, taking a step back and wiping her mouth with the back of her hand.

"Okay, forget I did that."

Not that he would be able to, at least no time soon.

"Please make sure it doesn't happen again."

"I doubt it will, not with that kind of reception. Okay, let's meet with this personal shopper and get it over with."

He made a mental note to find out all there was to know about Kennedy Fitzgerald. You could always find something if you dug deep enough.

Knowledge was power. He would be the one in control.

"Thank you for joining me on such short notice," Salim said to the executives gathered in the boardroom.

"I'm going to keep this meeting brief. As you've heard, my father is recovering from surgery and until he's fit to come back, I will be assuming his role."

So far, so good, Salim was following the script just as she'd coached him.

The senior management team seated around the horseshoe-shaped table remained silent as they digested the news. From the expression on many of their faces, it was clear that Salim was the last person they'd expected to step in. Some were smart enough to remain expressionless. Mark Wallingford, the executive Kennedy had met earlier, was the first to speak up.

"Salim, we're here to support you. You can count on this team."

"Yes, we'll help with anything you need," the younger man seated closest to Salim said.

"I'll need to get on your calendar," the only female in the room quickly added. She was an attractive, light-skinned woman in an elegant pantsuit and Kennedy watched her carefully.

"Give Diane a call and she'll put you on my calendar," Salim said, shooting her a tight smile. "Everyone should book time with me and do so before the end of the week. Come prepared to discuss any pending projects."

Kennedy's fingers were crossed under the table. So far, so good. It had taken a lot of coaching to get Salim here. His style of leadership was more relaxed than formal. He would be facing a much tougher audience shortly—the rank and file so better to establish himself as the person in charge.

She sat back observing the body language of the people surrounding him. The players were interesting. Most she'd already figured out were in it for themselves. So far Salim was doing a credible job of answering questions and issuing reassurances. No one would ever guess he hated the role.

Salim was dressed the part of the successful business mogul. The Nordstrom's personal shopper had excellent taste and a nice way with people. The tailor he'd brought along had worked like a demon to make sure his navy designer suit had that custom look. He wore polished black Cole Haan loafers on his feet and a light blue cotton shirt that worked well beneath his jacket.

When Salim balked at wearing a tie, Kennedy hadn't pushed the issue. In this industry he could get away with playing the part of the laid-back corporate executive, except that he'd absolutely refused to trade in his Timex watch for a Rolex. He said he'd had the Timex for almost twenty years and found it reliable. He did not need a fancier model.

Kennedy's eyes remained glued on the strong column of his neck. All that exposed coffee-colored skin peeking through the open shirt made her think of sex, something she hadn't thought of for quite some time. She'd never met anyone quite like Salim, unaffected by money and material things. A man with his wealth usually thought he could buy and sell people.

A ripple of laughter brought her back to the moment. Salim's closing comments must have gone over well. The executives seemed pleased as they headed out.

"I'll see you and the rest of the team at the town hall meeting," Salim called to the group as they filed out.

"I'll be there," the female executive who'd been flirting with him answered. "We should make ours a lunch meeting."

"I'm expecting everyone to be there," Salim said, ignoring the last part of her comment and setting the boundaries for what he expected from his management team.

Kennedy was proud of the way he was handling himself. *Working with Salim might not be so bad after all.*

Chapter 7

"I want you to find out everything you can about Kennedy Fitzgerald," Salim said to the detective seated across from him several days later.

Phillip Campbell had the face of a bulldog, but he'd come very well recommended. He sat jotting notes. "How deep do you want me to dig? We can go the route of what's solely public record, or I can look into previous relationships, financial standing, properties owned, that kind of thing."

"I want to know everything there is to know about that woman and I'm willing to pay top dollar. Specifically I want to know if Kennedy Fitzgerald has a history of being involved with married men of means.

I want to know if she's a gold digger or if she simply uses men to advance her career." Salim handed the detective a folder he'd put together. "In here you'll find copies of all the documents Fitzgerald signed when she was hired on. Several have her Social Security number. It should make it easier for you to run a background check."

Phillip wrapped a large paw around the folder before setting it down in his lap. "I can also have Ms. Fitzgerald tailed if you like."

"I don't think that's necessary. I'm fairly sure she's involved with my father, but given his illness I don't think there's any danger of them continuing their relationship soon. On second thought, it might not hurt to tail her. I'm curious if there's another man in the picture and if she's running a scam. Do you have everything you need?"

"I believe I do," the detective said, standing and shaking the hand Salim held out.

"Okay, Phillip. We'll touch base next week and you can let me know what you've found out."

After the detective left, Salim focused his attention on the bank of TV monitors on the far wall. There were still several shows filming and he realized how late it had become.

He spoke into the intercom. "Hey, Di, can you get Kennedy for me?"

"Sure thing."

Within minutes, Kennedy stood before him. "Was

there something you wanted?" she asked, appearing preoccupied.

"Yes, I was hoping you could have dinner with me. There are a number of things we need to go over."

Kennedy glanced at her watch and seemed to debate. "Well, I…"

"This is strictly a business meeting," Salim hurriedly assured her. He shut down his computer and stood.

"It's just that I'm having problems with my water heater. I'd hoped to get home in time to get someone out to take a look at it."

"I'll look at it for you," Salim offered.

"You would?"

Incredulity registered on her attractive features as if she couldn't picture him getting his hands dirty.

"I'm actually quite handy," he assured her. "And I enjoy fixing things. That's another reason this desk job is making me crazy. All you need to do is feed me and I'll see what I can do."

"It's a deal," she said, turning away. "I'll go get my stuff and meet you in the parking lot. You can follow me in your car." *Well, that's nice of him. Maybe after all his insults he's trying to call a truce. I'm game.*

On the highway as she was heading home, her cell phone rang, startling her.

"This is Kennedy," she said.

"I can hardly keep up with you," a sexy male voice said into her ear. "Do you always drive like a demon?"

Kennedy glanced at the speedometer. She was doing well over eighty and didn't realize it. A look in the rearview mirror did not yield the battered pickup truck she'd seen Salim get into. She'd wondered why he would drive a truck instead of the company-issued Lexus, but she'd come to expect the unexpected from the man she'd been hired to clean up.

A blast of a horn prompted her to look at the lane next to her. Salim's truck was beside her. He tooted the horn again and waved. She accelerated and switched lanes, getting in front of him before slowing down. When she pulled into the triplex's driveway, he was right behind her.

"Nice neighborhood," he said, getting out and looking around at the well-kept homes surrounding hers.

Kennedy nodded her agreement.

"It wasn't always this way," she answered. "The area was ripe for gentrification and I got in before prices hit the ceiling."

"You own the entire building?" He sounded surprised.

"Yes, I do."

She led him up the stairs and into her neat-as-a-pin unit.

"Your home is just like you," he said, looking around at the white-on-white walls and her beige carpets. "Everything's organized and scrupulously maintained."

Funny, but she didn't feel at all organized lately. Her life was way out of control. She was barely managing.

"Let me give you the grand tour," Kennedy offered.

"I'd like that."

Kennedy whisked him through the twelve-hundred-square-foot unit, secretly seething as he poked fun at her pristine kitchen. He opened a cabinet and peered inside, commenting on her neat little labels for everything. "Gawd, you *are* anal."

"I like it this way," she said, refusing to let him rile her. *He's here to help you.*

"Are you expecting someone?" Salim asked, tugging at the white tablecloth in the dining nook and rattling her china. She always kept her table set. It just made life easier.

"Let me show you the water heater," Kennedy said, keeping her voice even.

"Okay."

She entered the laundry room with him right behind her, and opened louvered doors.

"Is it too much to expect you to have tools?" he asked.

"Try the top shelf. I'm not sure what's in the box, though. I've had no occasion to use it."

He immediately reached for the box, opened it and began taking inventory of what was inside.

"Rustle me up a beer. I'll take a look," Salim ordered.

"I don't have beer. I have wine."

"Forget it. Water, then."

By the time she returned with his water, he had his sleeves rolled up and was elbow deep in grease. Just the sight of those corded arms made her wonder what the rest of him was like. She had to touch him. Kennedy reached over and erased the smudge on his cheek.

"That feels good," he said, smiling. "Try it again." He turned the other cheek.

Kennedy handed him his water.

He gulped the liquid down in a couple of quick swallows. "What's for dinner?"

She hadn't given that much thought. She doubted he would appreciate a salad; she was betting he was more a meat and potatoes guy.

"Pizza," she said, thinking quickly. "I'll order a pie and maybe I can convince the place to deliver beer."

"Get extra cheese, mushrooms and sausage while you're at it," Salim ordered.

"Consider it done."

She paid the deliveryman by credit card and returned to the kitchen to find Salim washing up.

"Okay, break it to me gently," she said, placing the pizza box on the counter.

"It's not good. The water heater unit is probably as old as this triplex. I'm no expert but I think you need a new one."

Kennedy sighed loudly. Just what she needed, to lay out more money; money she didn't have. At least not yet. She refused to think about it now.

"Let's eat," she said, motioning to the counter where she'd set out napkins and plates. The restaurant had delivered a six-pack of beer and she handed one to Salim, then popped one open for herself. She hated beer, but right now she needed something stronger than water.

"This is what I'm thinking," Salim said when he was down to only the crust on his pizza. "I'll call my mother's housekeeper and find out who our technician is. I'll have him come out first thing tomorrow and TSW will pick up the tab. It'll be your signing bonus."

She wanted to say she couldn't possibly accept, but who was she to look a gift horse in the mouth? Kennedy threw her arms around his neck and kissed his cheek. He moved his head slightly and she connected with his mouth. Now they were up close and very personal.

"That would be wonderful. Thank you. Thank you," she said against his mouth.

Salim swept her up into his arms and gave her a passion-filled kiss. She kissed him back with fervor, her hormones revving way out of control.

Her hands roamed his sinewy arms, then came to lie on the hard muscles of his chest. She pressed against him, drinking in the musky, masculine scent he put off, grease combined with male animal.

When Salim began kissing her neck, her common sense kicked in. He was technically her employer and crossing the line would be something they'd both regret.

"What's wrong, hon?" he asked in a hoarse voice. "Why are we stopping?"

"Because it's not a good idea. We shouldn't be doing this."

"Why not?"

"Because I work for you. It could get uncomfortable."

"To hell with uncomfortable. Tell me you don't like what I'm doing."

His lips grazed the side of her neck, nipping and sucking. She was pulsing all over uncontrollably and her brain shut down.

Kennedy's fingers dug into Salim's back, squeezing and kneading the hard muscles. His hands were on her butt now, bringing her closer to him until she could feel his hardness and hear his raspy breaths in her ear. The feel and smell of him excited her.

"I want to make love to you," he said gruffly.

"We shouldn't."

"Why not?"

"It's impulsive and irresponsible and you probably don't have protection." It was the first excuse that popped into her mind.

"Stop being so damn reasonable. Do something impulsive and wild for once," he urged. He patted his pocket. "I have a raincoat."

Wild? Spontaneous? Not in her vocabulary. People hooked up these days without thinking a thing about it. Did they do it with their boss, men they'd been hired to groom? If things went south she would be out the door faster than you could say "Microsoft."

Kennedy kept her hands against his chest, pushing slightly.

"We have to work early tomorrow. You have a meeting," she reminded him.

"The night is still young." He slipped a finger between the buttons of her shirt. "Why don't you lose this?"

"Not a good idea."

Salim worked a couple of buttons free and a moan ripped from the back of her throat.

"Was that a 'yes' I heard?" he had the temerity to ask, pressing his lips against her exposed flesh and moistening her skin with his tongue.

She moaned in return. Salim's fingers walked her cleavage. Excited, she tugged his shirt out of his pants and then raked her nails across his back.

It was the only encouragement he needed. He had her up against the counter in seconds, sliding her skirt up to her thighs and using one hand to cup her wet mound. Kennedy sagged against him and continued to moan.

"Oh, baby, let me love you," he pleaded.

Before she could answer, he slid her underwear aside and began stroking her until she purred. He paused only to slide on the condom before slipping inside her.

Kennedy squeezed her eyes shut. This was madness. Enjoyable madness. She was letting her hormones dictate. His hands on her body made her feel alive and womanly, and she reacted as any red-blooded female would. She wanted him inside her.

Kennedy guided him to her pulsing hot spot. Salim entered her swiftly, filling her up. Her thigh muscles clamped around his, riding him. From her standing position her ankles hooked around his. They went back and forth until he ramped up the action and Kennedy raked her nails across his back. She cried out, wanting more of him inside her.

She was trembling, sweating, bucking and babbling at the same time while Salim pleasured her. Emotions and sensations swirled inside until she thought she would go out of her mind. With one final thrust and a simultaneous cry, they climaxed together.

Kennedy held on to him, hoping that the feeling of having him inside her would never end, but she knew that was unrealistic. Soon reality would return and with it a flood of regrets.

And she didn't do regrets.

Chapter 8

The next morning Kennedy was jolted awake by the ringing phone.

"Can you make it here within the next hour?" Salim asked, sounding harried. "Diane's down with the flu." He'd left her a little after midnight explaining he wanted to sleep in his own bed and give them space.

"Okay, I'll be there in less than an hour," Kennedy answered, wondering what this was all about.

True to her word, she arrived at TSW within the hour. When she entered, phones were ringing like crazy. Salim held two in his hand talking back and forth. He nodded a greeting, and Kennedy ignored the gigantic tremor that started in her core.

She tossed down her briefcase and picked up one of the lit lines. "TSW, may I help you?"

The minute there was a lull between calls, she offered a suggestion. "Why don't we call a temp agency and get someone in to handle the administrative bit."

"Now, that's a good idea. Why didn't I think of it? Diane must have numbers of agencies in her Rolodex."

Kennedy was already one step ahead of him, sorting through the index cards that Diane kept in a cubbyhole on her desk. She waved one at him. "Here's a name. Should I call?"

"Absolutely. Have them send over two people. We'll need both to keep up with Diane."

The temp agency was more than happy to accommodate TSW, and in fact would have sent over half a dozen people if she'd asked. The moment she hung up, Salim's hand wrapped around her elbow.

"Come into my office. I want to run something by you," he said.

An electric bolt shot up her arm, and her entire body felt the voltage. The memories of last night, when he'd touched her in the most intimate of places, made her blush.

Making sure the phones automatically went to voice mail, she followed Salim into his office.

"Yes?" she asked, taking the seat across from him, and crossing one stocking-clad leg over the other.

"I've been thinking about things. The studio needs to be taken in an entirely different direction."

"What exactly do you mean? Can you even *do* that?"

"It may mean a managerial reorganization and bringing in new blood. We'll need to take a good hard look at our ratings and make some tough decisions about renewing current contracts."

"What brought this on?" Kennedy asked, curious. Salim hadn't been particularly interested in TSW or its programming before. It now seemed a radical turn-around for a man who'd shown little interest in his father's television studio to now want to shake things up.

Salim tugged at his earlobe. "I just think it's high time we start producing a few shows that are educational in content. There's drivel on television and we're losing market share. The current wave is reality TV, so why not show our audience what that really means?"

She hiked an eyebrow at him. "Meaning?"

"Meaning I'd like to produce documentaries that speak to people. I want to film starving children in Ethiopia, AIDS victims in the Sudan, children who've been turned into sex slaves in Cambodia, wives that are set on fire in India because their dowries aren't large enough."

She loved the way he thought and that he was passionate and sensitive. But she owed it to him and his father, her real employer, to think of what this would mean to the business. What Salim was proposing could be disastrous if not executed well.

Kennedy uncrossed her legs and stood. As she moved over to the window she felt Salim's eyes traveling the length of her. She experienced another electrical jolt and heat settled in her loins.

"A change of direction is not going to go over well with the executive team," Kennedy said. "People get comfortable doing what they're doing."

"Then it's high time to shake some people up. Don't you think?"

She did not disagree with him. She had her own thoughts about the executive team. Many were clearly coasting, biding time until retirement while collecting nice, fat checks. Kennedy knew little about the television business, but ever since accepting the job, she'd made it her business to learn. She'd carved out an hour each day to visit the sets and watch the shows being filmed. She had yet to see anything fresh or innovative. TSW tended to play it safe.

Salim steepled his fingers and looked at her over the tips.

Those eyes. Those hands.

Salim continued. "I say TSW should be a trendsetter. For years we've been about mindless sitcoms and talk shows with little substance. Why not show our viewers what's really happening out in the world? We should be educating people and making them think."

What he said made sense, but she still had a responsibility to help him make the best business decisions possible. The changes he proposed would not go over well with a team of executives that had a "don't fix it if it ain't broke" attitude. He would need allies among them to execute change. Plus they were an entertainment studio, not an educational network like PBS.

"Perhaps you should run your ideas by Mark Wallingford," Kennedy suggested. "As your godfather he should be watching your back. What about Yolanda? She seemed to think you walk on water and would be receptive to anything you propose. And Leonard, your brother-in-law, should be your staunchest supporter."

"You are strategic and bright," Salim said, smiling at her as if she'd just handed him an Emmy. "Set something up with Leonard and Mark." He slid out from behind his desk and came to stand beside her. Lost in their own private thoughts, they stared out of the window and onto picturesque grounds.

Kennedy had kept promising herself to walk during lunch and explore the parklike settings. But lunch so far had been eaten on the run.

Salim's large hands wrapped around her shoulders. He turned her to face him. "If you were in my position, and had the ability to show the world the atrocities you'd witnessed, what would you do?"

His amber eyes were fired with determination, holding her captive, pulling her in.

"I'd do what I felt comfortable doing."

He swept her off her feet, twirling her around until she felt slightly giddy and off-kilter.

"Thank you for helping make my decision. TSW Studios is now officially headed toward the documentary business. I'll see what everyone else thinks."

He set her back on her feet and leaned over to kiss her. And damn if she wasn't kissing him back and pressing her body against his. They were in his office and this needed to stop.

She fisted her hands, laid them against his chest and pushed. Salim captured her hands in his and deepened the kiss.

Kennedy's pulse raced and an unfamiliar light-headedness that had to be vertigo took over. The tingling now began in her toes and slowly worked its way up. The everyday world came back into focus in the form of a ringing phone.

"That's my private line," Salim said against her mouth.

"Then you'd better get it."

"Couldn't come at a worse time."

Couldn't come at a better time.

Kennedy gulped air and took a step back when he released her. Still dazed, she outlined her lips with her fingers. Salim's kiss had stirred deep-seated emotions, and these unbridled feelings were something new to a person who'd worked at keeping them at bay. For so many years having sex just didn't feel good. And now it did.

Kennedy's focus for far too long was getting her career off the ground. The occasional date she'd been on was more about trying to have a social life and not about emotionally connecting.

"Salim Washington," she heard Salim say into the mouthpiece. "Yes, I'll send someone to get the temps. Thank you." He hung up the phone.

That someone meant her, unless he was planning on having one of the executive's assistants handle that task.

Putting space between them was a good thing, especially now.

"I'll go to the lobby," Kennedy volunteered.

"Would you?" Salim's eyes were already on the monitors on the far wall. He shook his head. "Just look at the crap we're making. It's mindless stuff."

"Some of those shows have high Nielsen ratings," Kennedy reminded him on her way out. "Should I set up a meeting with Mark and Leonard so you can have a discussion with them?"

"Sure. By the way, I enjoyed that kiss. You kiss like nobody's business."

Kennedy's knees felt slightly wobbly when she smiled back at him. A million emotions warred inside.

Common sense told her not to take Salim's words too seriously. He'd acted on impulse and her wayward hormones had ricocheted out of control. Kennedy kept a smile firmly in place as she exited his office.

The morning went by quickly after that. Kennedy worked alongside the temps, showing them how to operate the phones and take messages. She assigned light typing to some and in between kept an eye on Salim, making sure he got to his many meetings on time.

Remembering that he needed to meet with his godfather and brother-in-law, she gave Leonard Green a call. It was the first time she'd interacted with Leonard and after speaking with him she was left wondering whose side he was on.

"I'm really busy," he said. "Can't we postpone for another day?"

"I'm afraid that's not possible. Salim needs to see you and Mark at 2:00 p.m. sharp."

There was an audible groan on the other end. "Two isn't a good time for me."

"Then please call Salim and tell him that. He's instructed me to have you clear your calendar and be in his office at two," Kennedy said firmly.

"We'll see about that."

He slammed down the phone.

Almost immediately, Salim's private line rang. Since he wasn't in his office, Kennedy debated whether to pick up. He'd gone off to referee a dispute between two stars of a popular soap; both were vying for more camera time. The fighting had now gotten so bad it was affecting the rest of the cast and delaying filming. The director was at his wit's end.

The phone stopped ringing and started up again. Entering Salim's office with some trepidation, Kennedy took a deep breath and grabbed the receiver. "Salim Washington's office."

"Not you again," Leonard Green snapped, slamming down the phone.

What an awful man and such an egotist! Kennedy decided to leave Salim a note letting him know his brother-in-law was looking for him.

As she reached for a pen, she noticed a thick folder on the glass desk. A personal and confidential sticker showed her name.

She was tempted to flip through and see what it held, but her conscience got the better of her. But why would her file be on Salim's desk?

Salim's private line rang again, and automatically she reached for it.

"Salim Washington, please," a gravelly voice requested.

"I'm sorry, Mr. Washington's stepped out. May I help you with something?"

"It's Phillip calling with an update."

"Do you have a last name, Phillip?"

"I'll take it from here," Salim's deep voice said from behind her.

Kennedy swung around. Her free hand clutched her chest and without comment she handed over the receiver.

"This is Salim." His palm covered the mouthpiece.

"You'll have to excuse me, it's a private matter. Why don't you go home and give this technician a call?" He handed her a business card. "He can come to you whenever it's convenient for you."

"Thank you," Kennedy whispered, stopping short of hugging him.

Salim's attention was already back with the man on the phone.

"What's the latest?" he asked, the receiver pressed against his ear.

Since lingering and deliberately eavesdropping wasn't exactly Kennedy's style, she left. But what she wouldn't give to be a fly on his wall.

Chapter 9

"You'll definitely need a new water heater," the technician said, confirming Kennedy's worst fears. "The one you currently have is probably as old as the building."

"How much is that going to cost?" Kennedy asked, her fingers massaging her temples.

The man named a figure that seemed astronomical.

Kennedy groaned. "I'll have to take out a second mortgage to afford that. My bonus won't cover that."

"Look on the bright side of things," he said. "You're not going to have to pay a penny for labor. TSW Studios is picking up all my hourly wages. Didn't they tell you that?"

Regardless, she would now be beholden to Salim.

She didn't like the idea of having to owe anyone anything, even a favor.

"I can get you a heater with my contractor's discount," the plumber offered, tapping into her thoughts. "And I'll have the unit delivered directly to the complex tomorrow. All you have to do is write me a check."

It sounded like a good deal to her. This wasn't a frivolous expenditure, and given her dwindling bank account, she'd take any discounts she could get. She called Ed downstairs to make sure he would be available to let the technician back into the complex, and got out her checkbook.

After the workman left, Kennedy replayed the intimacy of last evening and the kiss she'd recently shared with Salim. The events still rocked her world and left her reeling. It had all been so unexpected. But it would be to her benefit to keep things in perspective. Two healthy adults had slept together; best to expect nothing more.

Salim was currently on a mission to make changes in the studio. Her job was to make sure that he appropriately represented his father. Kennedy had the feeling Tanner would not be pleased if his son made drastic changes. He'd expect her to reel him in.

Her focus needed to be on the incentive dangled before her. It wasn't every day you were offered a television program of your own. She couldn't risk getting romantically involved with Salim if she valued her job.

Maybe what she needed was a good run to get her

head clear. Exercising and keeping fit was something she preached during team-building exercises and it was time she followed her own advice.

Kennedy changed into sweatpants and sneakers, then changed her mind about running. Instead she would head for the gym. On her way, her cell phone rang.

"Hello, this is Kennedy."

Her brother Roosevelt's mellow voice filled her ear. "Hey, girl, glad I caught you."

"What's up?" Kennedy asked, navigating a particularly treacherous turn with one hand.

"Have you talked to Mom lately?"

Kennedy felt the tension settle like a knot in the back of her neck. "Should I have?"

"I'm concerned. She isn't sounding like a woman who's just returned from her honeymoon."

That didn't come as a surprise. Her mother's taste in men stank. She came off as together to the outside world, but Taiko had always attracted the wrong kind of men. Most of Kennedy's life had been spent dealing with the fallout from these entanglements.

No wonder Kennedy had developed excellent coping skills.

Kennedy and her brothers were the results of Taiko's first marriage. Three more marriages followed in rapid succession, and now the blended family consisting of numerous stepbrothers and sisters. It had made for a chaotic time growing up. Kennedy had soldiered through and been exposed to all sorts of dysfunctional behaviors, running the gamut from kleptomania to eating disorders, plus emotional highs and lows. Through it all she'd tried hard to remain normal.

One stepfather had begun using Kennedy as his personal punching bag, another molested her a few times until Lincoln and Roosevelt stepped in, threatening to take the coward out.

"Kennedy, are you with me?"

"I'm here. I'll call Mother and see how she sounds."

She'd done her best to let those ugly childhood memories go. Therapy had helped. Yet despite growing up in a chaotic world, she loved her mother and wondered what she'd gotten herself into this time around. This coming weekend she'd take a long-overdue trip to Yakima and see for herself.

Even the thought of a short visit put her teeth on edge. Staying in the house she'd grown up in would be way too painful. She'd have to figure something else out.

Two hours and a lot of sweating later, Kennedy left the health club. The vigorous workout had helped clear her head. She checked her messages and was surprised to find that Salim had called.

With some trepidation she punched in his number and waited forever for him to pick up. When she was about to hang up, his deep voice filled her ear and she actually felt her heart palpitate; a strange reaction to someone she had no intention of getting emotionally involved with.

"Hey," Salim said, "I'd thought maybe you hadn't gotten my message. I was just about to call you back."

"I'm just now getting out of the gym."

"What happened with the water heater?"

"Kaput! I'm going to have to buy a new one."

"Sounds like an expensive proposition, just what you need." He actually sounded sympathetic.

"I'll manage. I have to," Kennedy said, forcing herself to sound optimistic.

"Would a salary advance help?" he offered.

Kennedy was stunned by his generosity. Not that she planned on taking him up on it anyway. She still had a little money left in the bank, plus a dwindling emergency cash fund, and the last thing she wanted was to owe him more on top of everything else he'd done.

"Thank you, but I'll be fine," she assured him, and not wanting to sound curt, added, "It's very nice of you to offer."

"What are your plans for this evening?" he came back with, surprising her.

She couldn't think quickly enough. "Uh…"

"Does 'uh' mean you have none or are otherwise engaged?"

"I was heading home to take a shower."

"Come by my place afterward and we'll have a late dinner. We have a few things to go over."

It didn't just sound like an invitation. It sounded like a command performance to her.

"Why don't you come out to Bellevue?" she countered. She wasn't quite ready for his place, business or otherwise.

"Not a problem. I can be there within the hour. Is that good for you?"

"Make it an hour and a half." It would give her time to shower.

"I'll bring the meal unless you prefer to go out," Salim offered. "Do you like Ethiopian?"

"I like food in general."

Kennedy floored the accelerator all the way home. She needed to pick up a bit. She'd left clothes on her bed, and the dishes needed putting away. Afterward she jumped into the shower and then for the next half hour raced around trying to straighten up the place.

Exactly on time, the doorbell rang. Kennedy straightened the dishes she'd just set down in the dining nook, and lined up the knives and forks.

She pressed the button on the intercom and after inquiring if it was Salim, let him in.

Kennedy's hands were clammy and there was a buzzing in her inner ear while she waited. What was it with her?

A light knock signaled he was at her door.

She opened to find Salim awkwardly clutching a shopping bag in one hand and a bottle of wine in the other.

"Come in," she said, standing aside.

"Spotless as always," he pronounced, looking around and handing her the bag.

Kennedy set the containers on the counter while Salim wandered around the room with a wide grin on his face, inspecting the few knickknacks she had out.

She'd always loved her living room because it was uncomplicated and clutter free. Someone had once referred to her home as a vanilla cocoon.

Two mocha-colored couches were positioned around a coffee table. The mantel on the fireplace on the far wall held one of the few spots of color, the same tulips that were in the flower box outside. Kennedy had always loved flowers. They made her feel alive.

"You've already had the grand tour," she halfway joked, as he continued his roaming.

"Yes, but now I just want to get a better sense of you." He waltzed into her bathroom, leaving the door behind him open. *Did I leave hosiery and underwear out?*

Salim's fingertips swiped at the glass blocks of her shower wall, leaving smudges behind. He stepped back out into the hallway and began examining the lithographs on the walls. She'd inherited some; others she'd bought in Japan.

"These seem out of character with the decor," he said insightfully.

"My grandmother is Japanese. The framed prints were gifts and mean the world to me."

"As they should," he said in a voice with a teasing lilt to it.

Boldly he wandered into her bedroom. They hadn't made it that far last evening. He seemed relaxed and very much like the carefree man she'd first met.

"Ah, in here I may uncover some deep dark secrets."

"I don't have any."

"Everyone does. If you poke hard enough you can find out what most don't want you to know."

Did that have some double meaning?

Feeling a little uncomfortable now, she whisked him through her sterile bedroom and onto the deck outside. Redwood flowerpots still held some tulips on their last leg. She made a mental note to replace the fading blooms with geraniums. Summer was right on the horizon and it was time for a change.

Salim's hands were on the deck's railings only inches away from hers. He inhaled a huge mouthful of air and said, "There isn't another place like the Pacific Northwest. Every time I think about moving abroad permanently I change my mind. We're blessed with liberal thinking here and we embrace all kinds of people. Personally, I think we're unique."

"I love it in Seattle, too," Kennedy agreed, making a U-turn and leading him back to the dining room. "Don't you think we should eat?"

Salim began unpacking his containers, setting them out on the kitchen counter.

"Your home is comfortable and suits you," he said.

"I thought you were going to say it doesn't have a lot of style or imagination."

"Simplicity and order can be comforting, especially to a nomad like me. Everything I value can be packed into two suitcases."

"What, you don't get the itch to acquire things when you travel?"

He tilted his head, thinking. "Only when I see something that's special and different, then I buy it and put it in my storage unit. For the most part the contents of my house can be packed up in a few cardboard boxes, furniture excluded."

"But you have the means. Your money can buy almost anything you want," she blurted.

"True, but it's not about material things. I choose to use my money to help those less fortunate than me. Now can we eat? I'm starving."

He picked up a handful of containers and placed them on the table. Kennedy got out the serving spoons and forks.

"Put those back. Ethiopian food is meant to be eaten with your hands. Here, I'll show you." He began gathering up the utensils.

"You're an eccentric man," she commented.

"And you're an unusual woman, with an unusual name."

"Not that unusual. My mother gave me a president's

name for a reason. I think she hoped to live vicariously through me. I've always been ambitious, and I'm willing to work hard for what I want."

"And what is it you want?"

"Utter and complete control of my life, and that usually comes with having your own money. If you have enough of it, you can call the shots."

"That's not always true," Salim said cryptically. He plopped down a large piece of sourdough flatbread on her plate. "It's *injera* made with fermented flour."

"Looks interesting," Kennedy said, breaking off a piece. She was starving and her stomach was beginning to make gurgling noises. "My mother was a J.F.K. fan and she named me after the president she adored. My brothers Lincoln and Roosevelt were named for the same exact reasons. "

"Your mother's a history buff? She must be an interesting woman and very similar to her daughter."

Unsure how to take his comment, Kennedy looked at him.

"That was a compliment," Salim quickly explained. He plopped a spoonful of what looked to be stewed meat on her plate, following it with a dollop of split peas and greens that looked like lettuce. The concoction smelled delicious and made her stomach gurgle even more.

"Traditional Ethiopian food has no pork," Salim explained as she reached for a portion. "No, don't use your left hand, use your right. The Moslems think good and kind deeds are performed with the right. Use the *injera* to scoop up your food and I'll pour us some *tej*."

Kennedy followed his instructions. She was getting an education. "What's *tej?*"

"It's a honey wine and the perfect complement to what we're eating. Open up." When Salim popped a piece of lamb-wrapped *injera* into her mouth, Kennedy's taste buds exploded.

"Mmmm, this is to die for."

He smiled at her, openly flirting.

"In Ethiopia it's customary to feed the person across from you. You go back and forth take turns feeding each other," he said with a wide smile.

It seemed such an intimate gesture for two people who basically had no relationship.

"It's a way of saying you're thinking about that person," he said persuasively.

Kennedy couldn't imagine he'd given her more than the most cursory of thoughts, other than plotting some way to unload her so that he could go back to living his bohemian life.

The confidential file on his desk with her name on it suddenly popped into her mind. She was dying to ask him about it, but he would probably think she was snooping.

Salim surprised her by asking, "Tell me about your mother?"

"What would you like to know?"

"I'm thinking you're probably both overachievers."

"Not true. My mother's educated although not particularly ambitious. She's always felt she needed a man to validate her existence."

"And she neglected you," Salim said thoughtfully. "That must have hurt. Where was your father? Didn't he have any say-so?"

Kennedy took her time answering. Her father had always been a very sore subject. "I barely remember what he looked like. He abandoned us. My brother Roosevelt barely remembers him. Our house was a revolving door with more stepfathers or wannabe stepfathers passing through."

"That had to have been tough." Salim squeezed her shoulder.

She liked this compassionate side of him and would really welcome those strong arms around her. Tough was putting it mildly; he should only know half of what she'd been through. On the other hand, it had made her self-sufficient and determined never to depend on a man.

"You said something about wanting to talk to me?" Kennedy asked.

"Yes, I met with Mark. We tossed around a couple of ideas on how best to implement the programming changes. I need you to help me strategize."

"What did he think of the documentary idea?"

Salim's golden orbs raked her face. "Mark doesn't think they'll fly. He thinks it's too radical a switch. He feels the idea should be discussed with the old man before I make changes."

"That might be a good idea."

"The hell it is!"

Salim was up like lightning and pacing the room. "I'm supposed to be in charge. If I have to run to a sick old man to get his permission every time I sneeze, then I'm nothing but a glorified figurehead. If I don't hold my ground, that pompous group of know-it-alls will have me for dinner."

"They'll serve you up as beef stew," Kennedy said, trying to lighten the mood. She picked up the dirty plates and set them down in the sink. "Are we done?"

"For now."

Salim circled the room. She could tell from his clenched jaw just how upset he was. She wiped her hands on a dish towel and crossed over to join him, placing a hand lightly on his forearm. "Why don't you start off by introducing one documentary on a topic that's really important to you? Debut it at prime time and run segments three consecutive Mondays. You'll get a good feel for how it's being received. And you'll have the ratings to back you up should you get flack."

"That's brilliant," Salim said, stroking his chin with his free hand. "You're very different from what my old man normally hires. His ladies are usually big of breast and small of brain."

"Should I be insulted?" Kennedy answered, chuckling and not of the mind to defend herself. He'd gotten this notion in his head she was involved with his father, and thank goodness he seemed to finally believe the truth. The horrifying thought occurred that maybe he had her pegged as a woman who slept with powerful men to get ahead. She knew he no longer believed that when it came to her and Tanner. But did he think it about himself and her?

"It's a compliment," Salim said, grinning down at her and laying his hand over the one she had on his forearm.

The connection between them was powerful, electric and unexplainable. Nevertheless it was there.

When Salim leaned forward and brushed her lips with his, Kennedy's entire body quivered. She felt her breath catch. Seizing the moment, Salim quickly thrust his tongue into her mouth and deepened the kiss. Kennedy's toes curled.

She wrapped her arms around his neck.

"We can't do this again," she said against his mouth, and tried to step back. "We work together."

"Yes, we can. There's nothing in the world to stop us from kissing."

But deep in her heart of hearts she knew it wouldn't just end there. One or both of them would eventually want to take it further.

Chapter 10

Salim was quickly finding out his prim life coach, leadership consultant or whatever she was, was anything but prim. Even now he could feel her arms tightening around his neck as she nipped at his bottom lip and caressed his tongue with hers. His head told him this wasn't the smartest move; the woman might still be involved with his father. But his body told him otherwise.

Yet there was something about Kennedy beyond the physical that drew him to her. The information in her file had painted a picture of an ambitious survivor who'd taken admirable steps to get her life in order. He'd read the information from cover to cover.

Kennedy's father had abandoned her mother when she was five. She'd grown up with a succession of stepfathers. Her maternal grandmother, as she'd earlier confirmed, was Japanese and born in Kamakura, a coastal city thirty minutes outside Tokyo. She'd married an American serviceman and moved with him back home to Seattle. Taiko was their first child.

After getting pregnant, Taiko married Ken Fitzgerald her junior year of high school. She'd then gone on to graduate and get a college education. Three children later, they finally divorced. Kennedy was their only girl. And although Kennedy's mother had told her the story of naming her after a president, Salim wondered if it really was true. He suspected Kennedy might have been named for her dad, Ken.

She'd done well at school and excelled in two languages: Japanese and French. But noticeably absent from Phillip Campbell's investigation was any mention of romantic entanglements.

The scent of Kennedy's shampoo was driving him crazy. The feel of her flesh underhand practically called for him to ravish her.

She stepped away, putting a safe distance between them, her fingers outlining the lips he'd just kissed.

"We can't continue to give in to every urge we have," she said.

He took a step forward, narrowing the gap between them. "You're enjoying it as much as I am."

"I shouldn't be, but you fascinate me. You're somewhat of an enigma," she said, facing him. "You have all this money at your disposal, yet look at you." She gestured to his ripped jeans, faded T-shirt and soiled leather sneakers. "Most men would be flaunting what they have. They'd use every opportunity to tell anyone who would listen they were president of TSW Studios. Not you."

He liked the way her slightly upturned eyes crinkled at the corners. He wondered what she would do if he tugged on the draw-string of her pants and kissed the strip of bronze skin peeking out when she moved.

"I've always liked the simple life," he admitted. "I've never had the desire to be worshipped or have my ego stroked. My mother did enough stroking at home to put me off that kind of male/female dynamic for life. It made me realize what I definitely don't want in a relationship."

"And what is it you don't want?" Kennedy asked boldly.

"I don't want an insecure woman, someone who feels the need to kiss my butt to get what she wants. I want someone passionate about her beliefs and not looking to keep up with the Joneses."

"You want a clone," she said in her matter-of-fact way.

"Not exactly. I want someone with depth. I'm not about arm candy, never have been."

The smell of peaches was turning him on. It was probably Kennedy's skin lotion or that wonderful shampoo she used. An intelligent woman usually did that to him, and Kennedy Fitzgerald was as smart as they came. Smart and dangerously attractive. He'd found out that underneath all that outward composure was a very passionate woman.

She yawned, telling him not so subtly it was late. He should be heading home, but he wasn't quite ready to call it an evening. Tomorrow he was meeting with his godfather, Mark Wallingford, again. He hoped Mark could help get the management team—all primarily his father's cronies—over to his side. He also had an interview with a reporter from the *Seattle Times*. He'd accepted that interview against Public Relations' advice.

Salim looked at the upcoming interview as a good opportunity to get some publicity for the Haitian clinic. The project could use the exposure and desperately needed the funds.

Ignoring the signs Kennedy was tired, he made himself comfortable on the couch. Her surroundings calmed him because her home was the exact opposite of his. He didn't have a place for everything the way she did. His walls were colorful, alive and vibrant, and his discarded clothing hung over chairs for days.

"I'm meeting with a reporter from the *Seattle Times* tomorrow," he said, delaying his leaving.

Kennedy perked up. "When did that come about?"

"The reporter called last week and I agreed to do the interview."

"Does PR know about this?" Kennedy asked.

"Yes, Public Relations wants me to transfer the reporter over to them so they can handle the questions."

"And you're ignoring their advice," Kennedy said with her usual amazing insight. "Why?"

"Because this may be my one opportunity to get funding for the Haiti project. It's the poorest country in the Western Hemisphere and the clinic badly needs supplies. The doctors involved all volunteer their services."

"Tell me about this clinic," she said, easing onto the couch next to him.

For the next twenty minutes he told her about his visits to Cité Soleil, which was a shantytown. It was one of Haiti's worst slums and a constant reminder to him of how privileged he was.

"You should see the place," he said, his emotions kicking in. "The sanitation is awful and there are literally hundreds if not thousands of people who are HIV positive. Some even have full-blown AIDS. Imagine getting no medical attention because you can't afford to see a doctor."

It burned him up at times to feel so helpless. But money could only do so much in a foreign country with a bureaucracy that was convoluted.

"Forgive my ignorance, but I thought funding was no longer a problem," Kennedy interrupted. "Hasn't awareness of the virus increased, and doesn't most of the world have access to treatments and drugs?"

"If you're poor and without funds, getting medical help isn't that easy. The medication can be quite expensive and the side effects unpleasant. Antiretroviral treatments work well, but getting an ARV treatment to Third World countries is at times impossible. It's gotten very political."

"That's awful. It's human lives we're talking about here," she said with passion.

Salim's loud exhalation of breath indicated his concurrence. He so agreed with her. He'd never been good at spilling his guts, but for some reason he was talking nonstop. It was a relief to be sharing with someone else.

"I recently lost a very good friend," he admitted. "He was a volunteer who became infected after reusing a hypodermic needle. Unfortunately, he chose to stay on in the Sudan. If he'd been in the States and getting the proper treatment, he would still be with us. If he'd had new supplies, new clean needles this wouldn't have happened. There are over twenty-two medications in existence to control the HIV virus today. AIDS no longer means a death sentence. Yet he died, and all because of politics."

"I'm sorry," Kennedy said, taking his hand. "So sorry." She had tears in her eyes. "There must be companies willing to provide some financial support. They get a tax write-off, don't they?"

Salim nodded his head. "The foundation does

receive some assistance from the United Nations Global Fund, and of course there are grants, but money is still very much needed. Now that word of the clinic has spread, we're not able to treat the influx of people coming from all over. Sometimes the lines are half a mile long. People collapse waiting in the hot sun."

"That's just awful," Kennedy said, wiping the tears from her cheeks. "Here we are in the United States, land of the plentiful, and we're sitting here fat, dumb and happy, while others struggle to get decent medical care, things we take for granted."

Salim just had to hug her. He kissed the top of her head. "Life's not always fair, hon."

"You don't think I know it?" She sounded as if she was about to say something and then changed her mind. "Let's do a run-through of tomorrow's interview questions." She smothered another yawn.

He should leave. Talk about overstaying your welcome, but he really was enjoying being with her, speaking with her.

"Sure, if you want to," he said.

For the next fifteen minutes Kennedy tossed a number of unsettling questions at him. Some tested his diplomacy and patience, but when the barrage ended he felt totally prepared for just about anything.

"Maybe we should have some coffee," Kennedy said, rising and yawning again.

"I'd prefer tea if you have it."

Salim followed her into the kitchen watching her deft movements as she got out mugs and tea bags.

When Kennedy handed him the mug their fingers touched briefly. He felt an electric charge and a pull in his loins. The smart thing would be to gulp his tea and get going. But he couldn't bring himself to do that. He sipped his tea slowly and faced her. His fingers were still itching to yank on the string of her pants so he could trace a path with his tongue on that tempting inch of flesh that was exposed.

The ponytail she wore made her look young and carefree. She reminded him of a girl he'd sat next to in fourth grade that he'd had a huge crush on. The one that he'd let get away because he had bigger and better things to do, like his involvement with the environment.

What the hell? Why not seize the moment? They'd had a fun, relaxing time so far. They were getting to know each other. Salim reached out and playfully tugged the ends of her hair. Kennedy automatically reacted by tweaking his nose.

"Ouch, you got me good." He laughed.

As the horseplay continued, Salim kept touching Kennedy more and more, and soon they were going at it like two love-starved teenagers. Their kisses were deep, soulful and real. He felt connected and turned on as he'd never felt before.

His hands pressed against the base of Kennedy's

spine, pulling her into him, his hardening member rubbed against her. She was not resisting.

Kennedy wound her arms around Salim's neck until they were so close he could feel her breath graze his cheeks. The tips of their tongues touched and intertwined. He was slowly spiraling out of control. Backing her up against the counter, he worked a button free and buried his nose in her clavicle. All he could smell was her scent. Kennedy's hand reached down, cupping him. Fingers rhythmically stroked.

Reserve and any semblance of common sense fell to the wayside. He slid a hand across her breast, his thumb slowly rotating around the nipple. Kennedy emitted a long, drawn-out groan. He kissed her again, letting his tongue play around the insides of her mouth. His ringing cell phone brought reality back home.

"You'll need to get that," Kennedy said in a breathy voice, pushing away from him.

"Damn phone. I thought I'd shut it off."

He looked down at the dial, registered the number and quickly picked up. "Yes, Mother, is something wrong?"

Lucinda was sobbing so hard he could barely hear her. The wrenching noise went directly to his heart.

"Talk to me," he pleaded.

"Your father…he's…taken a turn for the worse."

The sobbing began again, this time louder.

"Put Christiane on."

His sister came on the phone in seconds.

"Salim, Dad's had another attack. It's not good."

"I can be at the hospital within the hour," he said, without a moment of hesitation. Regardless of his personal issues with his father, he didn't wish this on anyone. His mother and sister would need his support.

By the time he hung up, Kennedy was already buttoned up and hovering.

"You need to go," she said, pushing him toward the door.

"Yes, I do." Salim tucked his shirt back into his pants and took a deep breath to steady himself. He needed to tell her something. "My old man's had another attack. I'll call when I find out more."

Kennedy gave him a tight hug. "Have faith. It'll be all right. I'll say a prayer."

"Faith is something I live by," he said, though lately it had seemed to be working against him.

"Call me, no matter how late it is."

"I will," Salim promised, kissing her cheek. "Try to get some sleep. To be continued."

Despite their tense relationship, he didn't want his father to die.

After Salim left, Kennedy thought about how close they'd come to making love again. Letting things get so out of hand was the stupidest thing she'd ever done. Everyone knew you didn't mess with the client. And she'd done something even dumber, she was starting to fall for the man despite his rough edges and the knowledge that he had no interest in settling down.

That was a huge problem and one she planned on getting over. Under absolutely no circumstances could she get intimate with Salim again. What she needed was a distraction. Kennedy checked her watch and thought it might be too late to call her mother. Yakima was one of those cities that rolled their sidewalks up when it got dark. But ten-thirty in the evening wasn't that late. She picked up the phone.

When a male voice answered she gritted her teeth. "Jack, it's Kennedy, Taiko's daughter. Am I calling too late? We haven't yet had the opportunity to meet."

"Hey, love, yeah, I heard you were back in town," the man slurred.

Kennedy sucked in her breath. Her mother deserved so much better.

"Yes, I'm back. Is my mother there?"

"She's in bed but you and I can talk."

"Would it be possible to wake her up?" Kennedy persisted. "I need to let her know I'm coming for a visit."

"About time. Let me see if she's awake."

Kennedy swore she heard him take another slug of what he was drinking.

"I saw pictures of you, missy. You're a pretty little thing."

The hairs on the back of Kennedy's neck rose. This was more of the same, except now she was older and wiser and didn't need Lincoln or Roosevelt to step in.

"Could you please check and see if Mom's awake?" she insisted.

"Of course, sweetie."

Lincoln and Roosevelt had already taken out bets on how long this marriage would last. Maybe they'd been too optimistic.

Taiko finally came on the phone; her voice sounded fuzzy. Had she been drinking too or crying? "Hey, baby."

Kennedy preferred to believe she'd been asleep and not crying. The marriage was far too new to already have these problems.

"Hi, Mom. Am I calling too late? What are your plans for next weekend?"

"None right now. I'll need to talk to Jack, though."

Kennedy explained she'd been thinking of visiting.

"Jack's really anxious to meet you," her mother said. "We'd like it if you stayed with us."

Not if she could help it.

"I'll call in the middle of the week to firm things up," Kennedy said, about to hang up.

"Did you ever get a hold of Marna or that friend of hers?" Taiko inquired.

"No, not so far. What have you heard?"

"She and that Alaskan boyfriend are supposed to

be back in Seattle. I would have thought she would have called."

"Haven't heard a thing."

"I'll see if I can get a number. See you next weekend, hon. Please don't disappoint me."

Kennedy hung up now determined to make the trip to Yakima. She was anxious to see what was going on with her mother. Not that Taiko would ever listen to anything she said.

But she was her mother and it was worth giving it a try.

Chapter 11

"You can go in," Diane said, gesturing toward Salim's open door. "The reporter from the *Times* should be arriving shortly."

Kennedy had been surprised when Diane called stating Salim wanted her to sit in on the interview. She'd wondered why her and not someone from Public Relations. But Diane had insisted she was just the messenger, and Kennedy had dropped everything and come running.

They'd done a quick rehearsal, going over and over some sticky questions. Kennedy had coached Salim on how to professionally yet evasively answer some of the trickier questions. Deciding enough was enough, they'd chatted about nothing in particular.

Salim's attention was on his e-mails when she entered. Kennedy used that opportunity to surreptitiously scrutinize him. She tried not to replay the events of the last few evenings, although that was virtually impossible. He'd been such an attentive and caring lover that just thinking of some of the things they'd done made her hot.

Underneath that elegant gray suit was a wild man. His hard body had felt right pressed against hers. His calloused hands had stirred up feelings that she'd suppressed for far too long.

Kennedy had often thought of herself as low on the sensuality meter. It was a mental thing really and had to do with her not wanting to lose total control. Losing control meant she was powerless to make well-thought-out decisions. Yet she'd allowed her freaky side to come out and that scared her.

Kennedy gazed out the window hoping the cooling breeze would soothe her burning cheeks. The temperature was easily in the seventies. When her glance returned to Salim she smiled at his bare feet. He'd kicked off his expensive loafers worn with no socks and wiggled his toes at her.

"How's your dad?" Kennedy asked, because she needed to stay on safe ground.

"Holding his own."

Tanner Washington's medical condition had been deemed newsworthy and all the major papers had carried updates on his health. Even TSW had been forced to make a brief mention of it during their morning shows.

"He may need a heart transplant or major surgery," Salim went on to say. "But the first priority is to get him stable and healthy enough to undergo that kind of operation."

"Please tell your dad I asked about him and give him my best," Kennedy said, her hand touching Salim's upper arm.

He gave her a hard look. One she didn't quite know how to interpret. Salim couldn't possibly still think she was involved with his father, not after what had happened between them. *I thought he was over that!*

"Nervous about the upcoming interview?" she asked, switching the topic.

"More like apprehensive. I'm more concerned about the meeting afterward," he said with amazing candor.

"You'll be fine. As for the reporter, just stick as close to the truth as you know it. That way you won't trip yourself up. I'd think you'd have a couple of supporters among the executive team. Your godfather and your brother-in-law should be watching your back."

Salim snorted. "I'm not so sure about that," he said, stopping short of fully explaining.

"Bryna Sullivan of the *Times* is here," Di said, sticking her head into the office. "Shall I bring her in?"

"Yes, of course."

Bryna entered, handing them both her card. She was average in stature, the kind of woman who blended in easily and you wouldn't give a second look. The only memorable thing about her was the red-framed glasses perched on the end of her nose.

"Please have a seat," Salim greeted, waving Bryna into one of the comfortable wingback chairs positioned in front of the monitors. He gestured to Kennedy to take the other.

The reporter's eyes roamed around his spacious quarters. She removed a miniature recorder from her purse and set it on the coffee table. "Would you mind if I taped our interview?"

Salim's glance locked with Kennedy's. Kennedy shrugged and mouthed, "Why not?"

"Go for it," Salim answered, smiling pleasantly and crossing a leg at the ankle, revealing that he wore no socks.

Kennedy swore the reporter smirked.

"Let me know when you're ready," Bryna said, depressing a button on the machine. Her eyes remained on Salim's bare ankles.

"All set." Salim's jaw was set tight and his shoulders were rigid. He was not as relaxed as he came across.

Bryna started off asking the usual questions like, where he'd gone to university. What he'd majored in, et cetera. She inquired about Tanner's condition and how

Salim felt about being thrust into a position of responsibility.

He was at his most diplomatic when he answered. Kennedy noticed he was slowly beginning to relax. Questions that were controversial got the briefest of answers.

"Did you want to take on the huge responsibility of being the head of a studio?" Bryna asked, looking carefully for a reaction.

"Actually, no. I was very happy doing what I was doing," Salim said.

"And what was that?"

He used that opportunity to plug the various charities he supported.

"There is one cause that I'm especially committed to," he added. "There's a foundation my partner and I created that could use additional funding. We're reaching out to the public and soliciting medical volunteers to help. The AIDS clinic we built is located in Cité Soleil, Haiti, one of the worst slums in the Western Hemisphere."

"I'd like to hear about this foundation and clinic in Haiti," Bryna dutifully said.

Salim jumped on that opportunity, making an all-out appeal for funding and volunteers.

Bryna shrewdly brought him back to the purpose of her interview.

"You've never really been involved with the television business before," she said. "How can an international business relations major make critical decisions affecting the running of a television studio?"

It sounded like a major putdown to Kennedy, but Salim thankfully kept his cool.

"Television is a business," he said. "And like any other business, what drives it is the bottom line. My experience managing a foundation isn't that different from running a profit-based company."

Bryna rubbed the tip of her nose and her glasses shifted. She used her finger to steady them. "Could you elaborate?" she asked.

"Running a studio effectively is all about making informed decisions. It's about knowing your demographics and keeping up on what's current."

One of Bryna's bushy eyebrows rose. "And you're that experienced in selecting shows that would be prime-time hits?"

A muscle in Salim's jaw twitched. Kennedy could tell the woman was starting to annoy him. She shot Salim a warning look. Now was not the time to get rattled or bent out of shape. The interview had gone well so far and he would lose all his credibility if he came off as a loose cannon. Bryna, shark that she was, would make mincemeat of him. They'd rehearsed a version of that question together. He knew how to ace it.

Come on, Salim, you know how to handle this one.

Salim stroked his chin. His eyes never left the reporter's.

"TSW has a proven executive team," he said. "These are people I rely on and trust. We're the fifth-ranking studio and we currently have five series that are prime-time hits. My goal is to elevate our position so that in the next year we'll be one of the top three studios. That can only happen if the right choices are made."

Kennedy wanted to kiss him. Salim had come through with flying colors.

"How are you going to accomplish that?" Bryna asked in her forthright manner. She nibbled the top of her pen while looking him over.

He chuckled as if it were a done deal. "Now, that one is easy. The studio is about to do something completely cutting edge. We're on the verge of introducing reality shows with a new spin."

"I'm intrigued."

The intercom buzzed.

"Yes, Di?" Salim inquired, listening for a while. His expression immediately becoming more guarded. "Tell Phillip I'll get back to him within the next fifteen minutes. I have his number."

He stood, signaling the interview had ended. Bryna tucked the recorder in the purse she'd slung over her shoulder and prepared to leave.

"Did you get everything you needed?" Salim asked, walking her to the door.

"Yes. I'll call if I have other questions."

"You'll let me know when the interview will run, then?" He shook the reporter's hand.

"I will."

The minute the door closed behind her, his body visibly sagged.

"How did I do?" he asked Kennedy.

"You were awesome. Now let's hope she publishes what you actually said."

Salim snorted again. "I haven't met one reporter who will quote you verbatim. I did get in a good plug for the clinic and foundation, and that's what I was hoping to do."

He reached for the receiver. It didn't take a rocket scientist to figure out it was time for her to leave.

With a wave in his direction, Kennedy headed off. She couldn't help wondering who this Phillip was. Why did Salim drop everything to take the man's calls?

With Kennedy out of sight, Salim punched in the detective's number. He answered on the third ring.

"Phillip Campbell here."

"Hi, it's Salim Washington. Do you have something new for me?"

"You may not be ready for this."

"Just spit it out."

"Your lady's almost broke," Phillip said.

Now, that surprised him. Salim remained silent, waiting.

"I ran a credit check on Kennedy," the detective volunteered. "Her home was a few days short of foreclosure before she finally paid the mortgage. Her utilities were close to being cut off, and would you believe her car was repossessed and sold at auction? As for credit cards, she's lost a few."

"Hmmm. Doesn't sound like the woman I know. We are talking about the same Kennedy Fitzgerald, the one with the middle initial A?" Salim had discovered Kennedy's middle name when he flipped through her personnel file. There must be a story behind Alexandra because that's what her parents had named her.

Just to be sure, the detective repeated Kennedy's Social Security number and some other vital statistics.

"I'm positive this is the same Kennedy Fitzgerald," he said. "She's got little or no money in the bank and she's been dodging creditors for months."

That could very well explain why the interest in his old man. A woman who was nearly flat broke would be desperate. She'd view the studio president as her only way out. Something about this whole business bothered him. The more he'd gotten to know Kennedy, the more certain he was that she wasn't some ho or gold digger.

"Do you have enough or would you like me to continue digging?" Phillip Campbell asked.

"Keep at it. Find out all you can about the woman. Get me something I can use."

Phillip chuckled. "That's what you pay me big bucks for, boss. I aim to please."

After he'd hung up, Salim prepared for his next meeting. The management team would not like what he had to say, and most likely his brother-in-law would be the most resistant.

Salim wasn't sure about Mark, either. While he came across as affable and supportive, Salim couldn't be sure whose corner he was in. Mark was the vice president of Program Development, which made Salim wonder what he'd been doing with his time. TSW's programming wasn't exactly innovative. Any suggestions to improve programming would be stepping on Mark's toes. His godfather would just have to get over it.

He'd just have to be both tactful and diplomatic when he had this conversation. Stabbing a finger at the intercom, he summoned Diane.

"Get Mark Wallingford on the phone, and tell him I need to meet with him now," he said. "Delay my next meeting if you have to."

"I'll get on it immediately," Di said in her usually efficient manner.

While he waited, Salim mentally rehearsed the conversation. Visions of a nude Kennedy Fitzgerald kept popping into his head. He squeezed his eyes closed, shutting out the erotic images.

His full concentration needed to be on the upcoming meeting. It might very well turn out to be an uncomfortable conversation.

Chapter 12

Salim made dinner plans with his mother and sister for later. Christiane had found a sitter for his two nieces and the two of them had somehow managed to coax their mother into taking a break from her bedside vigil. She of course planned on calling the private nurse every half hour to get an update on her husband's condition.

He'd chosen a modest but popular seafood restaurant for them to meet. Christiane complained the chain restaurant wasn't fancy enough, but Salim had said, "Tough." The place served decent food and he was not out to impress anyone.

His mind was still on what to do about Kennedy when he pulled into the parking lot. She continued to fascinate him. It would be interesting to see what Phillip, the detective, could further dredge up.

Salim had glanced through Kennedy's personnel file and been intrigued that she had a master's degree. She also spoke three languages, one of them being Japanese.

Kennedy had explained her exotic looks when she'd mentioned her maternal grandmother was Japanese. Even now he could still picture her flushed face as he'd made love to her and the way her body moved. Why was he wasting time thinking about a woman who didn't mean that much to him?

"Salim!" his sister called, waving to him. She stood in front of the entrance of the seafood restaurant. "How come you're all dressed up? Oh, I almost forgot. You're the president now."

The sarcasm was not lost on him. Christiane loved the entertainment business and had begged their father to give her a job, any job.

"Don't make fun of my monkey suit."

The studio had always been a bone of contention between them. To this day Christiane couldn't get over being slighted when her initial was omitted from the television studio's name. Tanner was somewhat of a chauvinist and he believed that men were born to run businesses while women stayed home raising children and taking care of the home. As evidence, TSW was sadly lacking when it came to female executives.

Christiane softened a bit, throwing her arms around him and enveloping him in a warm embrace. "Suit or no suit, you have *bad boy* written all over you. Why are you still driving that beat-up old pickup? Isn't a Lexus the standard company vehicle?"

"Don't make fun of Deka," he responded, laughing. "I love that truck."

"Deka. I forgot that wreck has a name." Christiane blew a wisp of hair out of one eye. She was used to being called Leonard Green's trophy wife, except she was no trophy. Salim strongly suspected that whatever innovative thoughts Leonard brought to the table as senior vice president of Business Affairs and Contracts at TSW were courtesy of Christiane.

"*Deka* in Somali means 'one who pleases,' and my truck pleases me. Where is Mother?"

"Inside and seated at the table. Her legs aren't what they used to be and you're late."

His sister linked an arm through his, guiding him inside. Sibling rivalry or not, they loved each other.

"You could have picked a nicer restaurant," she commented.

"What's wrong with Carson's?"

"It's hardly upscale. No tablecloths, menu on a blackboard. Mother's not used to slumming."

"Thank goodness Mother's not a snob," Salim responded, pecking his sister's cheek. "Carson's has an excellent reputation for seafood. They've got the best salmon, second to Alaska."

Salim looked around for a stylishly coiffured head of hair. He spotted his mother at a banquette at the back of the room. Christiane had picked the best table in the house, one with an outstanding view of the sound. In the rapidly growing darkness, twinkling white lights indicated there were still boats out on the water.

"Just look at my boy," Lucinda said, sliding from the booth to greet him. She was immaculately dressed in one of the St. John suits she favored. She eyed him up and down. "Forgive me for staring. I'm just not used to this. I wish I had brought my camera."

"Oh, Mother!" Salim rolled his eyes as he slid onto the other side of the banquette. Christiane took a seat next to her mother.

When Lucinda's cell phone rang her face crumbled. "I'm so sorry. I'm going to have to get this."

As she picked up, Salim unashamedly listened to the one-sided conversation.

"He's resting comfortably but asking for me you say—yes, yes, I'll cut short my dinner and get back— I can be there in half an hour."

Before she could hang up, Salim snatched the cell phone out of her hand. "This is Mrs. Washington's son, Salim. Is there a problem? It's not an emergency, then, good. Mother will be there when she gets there. I hate it that he has you calling every hour." He ended the conversation by closing the flip phone.

"Why did you do that?" Lucinda quizzed, her lips trembling.

"Because the old man's resting comfortably. The nurse just confirmed there hasn't been a change in his condition. You deserve a couple of hours of downtime."

Lately his mother looked old and worn. The worry lines around her mouth and eyes were even more pronounced than he remembered. Salim could kill his father for what he had done to her. He'd manipulated her since the beginning of time. God forbid if he wasn't the center of her universe.

It had always been the Tanner Washington show. Lucinda was so browbeaten that she could no longer offer an opinion without quoting his father. Tanner had tried inflicting his will on Salim, as well, but that always ended in heated arguments.

Salim had tried doubly hard not to model himself after his father. When the time came to settle down he wanted a relationship based on mutual respect and love. He was looking for an equal, a partner and not someone to control.

He would willingly bide his time until he found "the one." But until then, he would throw himself into the work that he loved; work that was meaningful. Helping people less fortunate than he. The woman involved with him would have to be on the same wavelength or they'd never make it. He didn't give a damn about money unless it was to be used to improve a life or make a difference.

"What's going on at TSW?" Christiane said, her eyes lighting up.

"Let's have a drink and then I'll tell you."

Salim gestured to the server to come over. He placed their drink orders.

"Things are running smoothly. Not a lot to report at this juncture. But my feeling is the studio needs to move into an entirely different direction."

"Your dad's not going to like change," Lucinda warned.

"Oh, Mom, change is good. When we resist we become dinosaurs," Christiane said astutely. She'd always loved the business and, truthfully, she would be a far better president than Salim.

Salim outlined his ideas. As he spoke, more and more thoughts came to mind. He could use his position to his advantage and he could use the studio to make a difference in several lives. Not a bad idea.

"Why are you grinning like a hyena?" Christiane quizzed, looking at him through narrowed eyes.

"No reason. I'm enjoying being out with my two favorite women."

"Sure you are," Christiane said. "You could have any woman you wanted."

The funny thing was, only one woman came to mind and she wasn't what he thought he would ever go for.

Salim's mother, who knew him better than anyone else, raised an eyebrow.

"He's up to something," she said.

"Better be something good," Christiane muttered under her breath.

It was all good. He was about to take TSW Studios in a cutting-edge direction, introducing documentaries to the prime-time world. It would be a far departure from the lighthearted, award-winning sitcoms the studio had built a name on.

Entrees and dessert ordered, they sipped on coffee.

"We should leave, Mother, you need to get to Dad," Christiane eventually said after they'd finished their meals, signaling to the waiter for the bill.

"What are you doing?" Salim asked.

"Getting the check."

"No, you don't. Dinner is on me."

Lucinda allowed herself to be led away.

Later that evening at the Washington estate, Lucinda was still awake and stretched out on a divan in the study. Christiane, after pouring them both glasses of wine, sat in a lounge chair facing her.

"I cannot believe my boy still won't make the time to look in on his father," Lucinda groused. "Sometimes I wonder where his priorities are."

"He did come to the hospital when we called him," Christiane reminded her mother.

"Yes, but he hasn't been back since."

"He's called quite often, Mother. He and Dad aren't exactly the best of buds. They've had their issues."

"That's beside the point. Salim should be able to get away for an hour to visit."

Lucinda saw things one way, Salim another. To her brother's credit, he was not a hypocrite. It was the thing Christiane loved most about him. He was real and not at all big on keeping up appearances.

"Maybe I'm the one who should be going into the studio," Christiane muttered contemplatively.

"You've got enough of a job raising two rambunctious toddlers."

"My kids are pretty self-sufficient and love their nanny to death. I was thinking of going in for a few hours each day and helping."

"And why would you do that?" her mother asked, sitting up.

"I could support Salim and learn the business from the ground up."

Lucinda's chin wobbled. "Leonard would never go for that."

"Screw Leonard. We're talking about me. It's time I did something useful."

"Don't rock the boat, baby," Lucinda advised. "Leonard's made a good life for you and the girls. He's a wonderful father and he adores you."

"My husband can be quite controlling at times. As

for making a good life for me and our children, he would be nothing if he wasn't employed by TSW. He hates working for Salim. He's used to being a big shot and running over everyone."

Lucinda's wagged her finger sagely. "You're being disloyal, baby. Every marriage has its ups and downs. The important thing is Leonard comes home to you."

Christiane rose and began to pace. "I want more from a marriage than a man who comes home to me at night. I could easily live off of my trust fund if I have to. I want a man who puts me and my children first. I want someone who appreciates my intelligence instead of treating me like some brainless trophy who doesn't know what's going on."

"But you love Leonard," Lucinda insisted, still looking shocked.

"Loving him and being realistic about what he's about are two very different things. I'm bored, Mother. It's time I put that expensive Ivy League education to work. I need to start using my brain again."

"Entertaining, keeping a nice house and raising two children is work," Lucinda reminded her.

The phone rang and her mother's body went rigid. Tilly came hustling in with the remote phone in hand. She had an ashen look to her face and her hands actually shook.

"It's the hospital, ma'am," she said, handing the phone to Lucinda.

Taking a deep breath, Christiane grabbed the receiver before her mother reached for it.

"Hello," she said, her heart palpitating wildly.

"Mrs. Washington?" a female voice quizzed.

"This is Mrs. Washington's daughter, Mrs. Green."

"We'll need you back at Swedish Medical Center as soon as you can get here."

"Is there a problem? My father…"

"The doctor would prefer to discuss the situation in person. Just come as quickly as you can."

"That is the most ridiculous thing I've ever heard," Leonard Green shouted at Salim. On returning to the office, Salim had called a late meeting.

"TSW isn't in the documentary business. I can understand you wanting to introduce new programming, but come on now, documentaries? That's limiting your audience. Those types of films attract intellectuals. That's not exactly prime time's target."

Several side conversations started up. Salim cleared his throat, and when that didn't work he stood up drumming his fingers on the desk before him.

"Okay, let's focus. If you have something to say, put it out there instead of whispering in little groups."

"Why are documentaries any different from the reality shows that are so popular?" Yolanda asked, bringing the meeting back to its purpose. "Wouldn't you just be taking reality in a different direction? Perhaps you could share more of your vision."

Yolanda had always been smart and outspoken. Salim was happy to have her on his side.

"What if we were to capture on film the experiences of a real person? Let's say we filmed a week in the life of an AIDS victim, or maybe the realities of living life on the street? We could do an entire segment about the treatment or lack of received by those with no medical insurance," Salim pitched.

"It sounds much too depressing to me," Leonard groused.

"It doesn't have to be," Mark Wallingford said gamely. "The message could be one of hope."

Salim quickly jotted a note.

"I like that. Documentaries with a hopeful message."

Several of the management team tuned in and even seemed excited.

His godfather had come through, backing him up. Earlier he'd been on the fence about the changes Salim suggested. Their previous meeting had ended with no assurances that he would support him, but now apparently he'd changed his tune.

"I'm probably the only one old enough to remember when everyone thought putting the Loud family on at prime time would be a real downer," one of the senior members of the executive team said. "No one thought anyone would want to witness a family air its dirty laundry. Yet that show was a trendsetter and way before its time. It got amazing ratings and drew a huge prime-time crowd. I'm with you, it's time to try something new."

The executive was known for being set in his ways. Was he really on Salim's side or simply kissing butt?

"Changing the format midseason will be a huge mistake," another of the men admonished. "I'd wait until next season before introducing any revolutionary concept. If we're going to put folks to sleep, let's do it in small doses."

There was a ripple of laughter quickly squelched when Salim shot a look the man's way.

"Okay, you come up with some fresh ideas for programming, or maybe you think we should continue to churn out the tried-and-true. If we're content being reactionary rather than visionary I'd prefer it not to be on my watch."

"What about market research?" one of the younger executives asked.

"What about it?" Salim came back. The man must think he was a fool, shooting from the hip without having his ducks in a row.

"Before we veer off our usual course, wouldn't it make sense to gauge the public's interest?" he tossed back.

A lively discussion followed with his brother-in-law, Leonard Green, taking the lead. Leonard spoke persuasively trying to sway everyone to his way of thinking.

"With all due respect," he said, "the current programming works, so why fix it if it ain't broke? TSW has been around for almost thirty years, it's almost as old as you."

There were a few more chuckles.

Confident he had his colleagues support, Leonard continued. "For more than a quarter of a century this studio has had an outstanding reputation. We've produced several hit shows and dominated prime time. Why shake up a winning formula?"

Kennedy, who was seated on the fringe of the group, shook her head frantically, signaling to Salim to keep his cool. But brother-in-law or not, he couldn't let Leonard usurp his authority. If he allowed anyone to run over him he would never gain their respect. His sister's husband was an obnoxious, controlling jerk. To this day it still boggled Salim's mind what Christiane saw in him. Maybe she'd needed a father figure when she married him. Tanner hadn't exactly been a model dad.

"That may be so," Salim said, chuckling along with the group to show he had a sense of humor. "But as a corporation we've grown stagnant. We're dinosaurs now. Not visionaries. Here's what I want you to do. Go home and think of a cause you're passionate about. Imagine you were given the leeway to film a documentary, or even a talk show on the subject. Think about what you'd like to see and what would perk your interest."

The door pushed open and Di stuck her head in the crack. She signaled time-out with her hands. "Sorry to interrupt. I need you."

Salim quickly ended the meeting and watched the relieved team file out, Kennedy included. Their expressions indicated they were still shell-shocked by what he had said.

"Okay, Di, what's so urgent?" Salim asked, trying to hide his trepidation.

Her eyes welled up. It was the first time he'd seen Diane show any emotion.

"Your sister called. She said I should find you wherever you are. She wants you to call her back."

That could mean only one thing: an emergency involving his father. Salim felt strangely off-kilter as he braced himself for the worst. For years he'd hated his father, yet the thought that he might be fatherless now left him cold.

"What else did she say?" he demanded.

Diane pressed the cordless phone into his hand. "Call your sister."

Salim waited until she'd left to make the call. He'd almost given up on anyone answering when his sister, sounding as though she had a whopper of a cold, picked up.

"Hey, what's up?" Salim asked, trying to keep his tone light.

"Salim, I really do think you should come to the hospital," Christiane pleaded with him.

"All right, just break it to me," he said quietly.

There was a slight pause, then, "Dad's had another

attack and he's barely holding on. The doctor said this time there was severe damage to the heart. I'm not sure he'll survive the night."

"How's Mom?"

"She's not good. All she does is pray and say that she wishes it was her, not him."

"I'll be there right away," Salim said, hanging up the phone.

"I'll drive you wherever you need to go," a female voice said close to his elbow.

He turned to see Kennedy standing there. He had no idea when she'd come back in. What he did know was that he'd never been happier to see anyone in his life.

She embraced him, rubbing his back as if comforting a child. He loved the feeling of her hands on his body, but right now his head was elsewhere. He rotated his neck, squared his shoulders and took a deep breath.

"What do you need? Your laptop, briefcase? What else?" Kennedy asked in her usual take-charge manner. "Give me your car keys and I'll drive, or if you prefer we can take my car."

"No, I'll drive," Salim insisted. "It will give me something to do. You can keep me company."

After giving Diane instructions to cancel the other meetings she'd set up for tomorrow just in case he wasn't in, they prepared to leave.

"Please keep me updated," Diane called after them.

"If there's anything at all I can do, don't hesitate to ask. No matter how late it is."

Salim drove like a demon all the way to the Swedish Medical Center while Kennedy sat beside him deep in thought.

Right now she sat quietly staring out of the window, sensitive enough to allow him the space he needed. Life could change drastically if his father didn't survive the night. He didn't want to think about that.

While he and Tanner had their issues and he'd wished him out of his mother's life, now that there was the possibility he might be, he felt guilty for having such thoughts. Salim was embarrassed that he hadn't made the effort to maintain an adult relationship with his father.

Regardless of how he felt, if it hadn't been for his father, he'd have no trust fund available. It was Tanner Washington's money that helped him save lives. But what good was that money if you didn't have good health?

In a reassuring gesture, Kennedy's fingers squeezed his thigh. Salim glanced down, cleared his throat and shifted gears. His pants all of a sudden felt very tight. His ancient pickup truck had always been a solid and reliable means of transportation and he found comfort in its predictability. Absentmindedly, he patted the hand that rested on his leg.

"We're almost there," he said out loud, further convinced that going to the hospital was the right thing to do. He needed to make amends with his father and make things right.

Kennedy gave his leg another firm squeeze. Now was not the time to have sensual thoughts about what he would like to do to her, not when his father might be taking his last breath.

Kennedy's soothing voice intruded. "Just a few more minutes and you'll see what's what."

After circling the parking lot they finally found a spot. Salim gulped in huge mouthfuls of air and climbed out of the truck.

Kennedy linked her arm through his. "I'm right here with you, hon. I'll stay as long as you need me."

Having her hand in the crook of his arm felt comforting. In an act of solidarity they approached the lobby information desk.

"We're here to see Tanner Washington," Salim announced.

The person managing the desk pushed some buttons on the computer and gave them directions.

They took an elevator up and headed down a long hallway. Christiane was at the end of the hall pacing anxiously. Her eyes were so swollen they were slits. Salim's heart clenched and unclenched.

He introduced the women. His sister nodded at Kennedy. Christiane threw her arms around his neck, almost strangling him.

"Oh, Salim, I'm so glad you're here."

He put her away from him and waited for the bad news. "Take a deep breath now."

Salim's skin felt clammy and there was a vice around his heart.

"Let me talk to the doctor. Where is Mother anyway, in the room with Dad?"

Kennedy turned away and started up the hall, giving them space.

"Dad's in a private room and Mom's not leaving him no matter what we say. She's already called our minister and I'm supposed to let her know the minute you arrive."

"You two get something to eat and I'll go in and see Dad," Salim offered. "I can spend the night here if you need me."

Christiane's eyebrows rose. "That's big of you. That means a lot." She paused. "Can't you swallow your pride and make peace with the man. Mother would be ecstatic and you would get rid of your guilt. This might be your only chance to tell Dad you love him."

Salim clenched his jaw so hard he thought the enamel might chip off his teeth. Christiane was asking him to put all the hurt and bitterness behind him and forgive a man he did not respect. But maybe it was time he let go of all that negative energy.

"Come on, let's go see our parents," he said, signaling to Kennedy that he would be right back.

His sister hugged him so tightly he thought he would pop.

"I'm so proud of you for doing the right thing."

He wasn't so sure what he was doing was right. He just knew it would make him feel better, and would make looking at himself in the mirror that much easier. If something happened to Tanner now, he would be able to live with himself.

And that's all that he wanted: a guilt-free life.

Chapter 13

Two days later Tanner was still hanging in there. His condition had been upgraded from critical to stable.

Salim was spending more and more time at the hospital which left Kennedy at loose ends. She busied herself organizing his office and strategizing the career steps to take once her gig was over with.

Much to Leonard Green's chagrin, Mark Walling-ford was now the acting president and not him. Mark was already putting out feelers for the kinds of documentaries the studio could produce, and Leonard's nose was definitely out of joint big time. The power plays were becoming more and obvious, leaving the executives divided down the middle; some supporting

Leonard, the others Mark. The whole thing had gotten ridiculous.

Some bigmouth had leaked to the media that TSW was about to introduce revolutionary programming. As a result the phones had been ringing and Public Relations had their hands full.

Kennedy was just about to pack it in for the day when Salim popped into her office. He'd returned from his latest stint at the hospital.

"How's it going?" he asked, giving her a wide grin. He looked so tired she wanted to hug him.

Kennedy felt an electric jolt ricochet up her spine. It was becoming a familiar reaction whenever he was close. She didn't want to believe she was falling and falling hard.

"The phones have been ringing off the hook," she said. "The world wants to know how your dad is, and of course rumors are floating around about the new programming."

Salim's voice registered his exhaustion when he answered, "Fill me in over dinner."

"I don't know if I can. I'm leaving for Yakima tomorrow. I need to go home and pack."

"What's in Yakima?"

"My mother and brother live in eastern Washington. I'm visiting my brother, his wife and new baby."

Rather than stay with her mother and her husband, Kennedy had decided to accept Lincoln and Shelli's kind invitation to stay with them. She was looking forward to playing with her niece, as well.

"Okay, you still have to eat. We'll have dinner at my place and you can brief me on the goings-on. I won't keep you out late, I promise."

While the prospect of going to Salim's home excited her, because she'd never been, she really needed to go home and pack.

"Look," he said, sniffing under his armpits jokingly. "Eating at home is a necessity. I'm not exactly restaurant material right now. I'm exhausted, smelly and could definitely use a shower. We'll get takeout, or order something in and discuss business, you can then go home and do what you need to do."

There went any fanciful notions that it would be anything more than a business dinner. Still memories of their last dinner together flittered through her mind, producing a warm and flushed feeling. Needing to keep occupied, Kennedy began gathering her things.

"Now that Diane's back, I've been helping her catch up with the administrative stuff," she said. "I've also been attending meetings and taking notes. I'll bring you up to date."

"Good, we'll go over them at the house. How's Mark handling things?"

"He's done a tremendous job of keeping the place running. By the way, David MacFarland has been by a couple of times to see you. He wants to get on your calendar. He keeps insisting it's urgent."

David was the volatile soap opera actor Kennedy had met during her first walk-through of the studio.

Salim groaned, took her arm and headed out. "These actor types are so high maintenance. David has to know I've been in and out. It's no secret my old man is ill."

"Something's obviously on his mind. He keeps coming back."

"Probably looking for more money. Each year his demands become more and more outrageous and the ratings just aren't there to support his expectations. I'll have to talk to Leonard to see if it even makes sense to renew his contract."

By then they'd reached the executive parking lot.

"This time you follow me," Salim suggested, hopping into the truck that stuck out among the sleek row of Lexus sedans.

They braved the evening traffic on Interstate 5 and headed north for Green Lake. That area, with its awesome water view, had always been one of Kennedy's favorites. It suited Salim's personality and lifestyle and was the perfect combination of suburbia and country living.

Salim's home turned out to be a beige craftsman's cottage with hunter-green shutters. It was perched on a cliff with a magnificent view of the lake. Flowers were beginning to bloom on the small patch of lawn as they walked under a budding arbor and up to his front door.

"What a beautiful home," Kennedy said as she entered and crossed the planked wooden floors. She paused to admire the skylights, then French doors leading to the outdoor deck.

"Thank you. It's the result of a lot of hard work, most of which I did myself."

Salim kicked off his shoes and shrugged out of his shirt. The T-shirt he wore hugged every inch of muscle. Kennedy felt her gut clench and her breath hitch. He set his cell phone on the coffee table and took off for the kitchen, returning shortly with a glass of wine and a folder.

"This will give you an idea of what my foundation is about. I'm off to take a shower. I won't be long."

He disappeared into the back and Kennedy made herself at home on the leather sofa. She browsed through the pamphlets and newsletters he'd handed her, and gazed at the numerous pictures of him. Many showed him working with his hands or at times speaking to large groups of people, but in each he was casually attired and looking relaxed.

Salim's foundation was aptly named HIV; the acronym meant Helping Infection Vanish. It did everything from feeding starving orphans in Third World countries to teaching adults the basics of good hygiene. Overall the primary focus was educating people on safe sex.

When Salim's cell phone jingled, Kennedy ignored it. It wasn't her place to answer. The phone stopped

ringing and the house phone shrilled. She waited for a
recorder to pick up and when it didn't, she reluctantly
answered. What if it was someone at the hospital trying
to reach Salim?

"Hello?" Kennedy kept an eye on the direction
where Salim had disappeared.

"Salim Washington, please," a man's deep voice requested.

"Can I tell him who's calling?"

"Phillip Campbell."

The name sounded familiar. She recalled a Phillip
calling Salim's private line. Was it the same guy?

"He can't come to the phone right now," she said.
"Does he have your number?"

"I'll take that," Salim said, coming up behind her.

Kennedy handed him the phone and returned to the
sofa. She tried not to eavesdrop although the bits she
could hear had her curiosity piqued.

"That's ugly," Salim muttered, sounding as if he
would bite someone's head off. "What do you mean she
was molested—tell you what, I'll talk to you in more
detail tomorrow." He hung up.

The bits and pieces she'd heard made awful
memories surface. Kennedy could still vividly recall
calloused hands exploring her most intimate parts. Re-
visiting that experience made her feel angry and jittery.
If it hadn't been for her two brothers picking up on what
one stepfather was up to, she'd be a basket case today.

Her mother initially refused to believe her husband was that kind of monster until the evidence said otherwise.

"So, what do you think?" Salim asked, taking a seat next to her on the couch and tapping the binder. He pocketed his cell phone.

"I think your foundation is literally a lifesaver. Who's running the show now that you're tied up with TSW?"

"Nate, my partner, is carrying the load in my absence. We have several seasoned volunteers pitching in, as well. Does Chinese sound good to you?"

"It sounds perfect."

Salim placed their order, and while they waited for the delivery, Kennedy briefed him on what was going on at the studio.

"It's been the classic case of too many chefs and not enough servers," she said, sighing.

"My sister, Christiane, wants to become more involved. She's going to start coming in for a few hours."

"Isn't she the one married to Leonard Green? I thought she was a stay-at-home mom."

"Yes, but she's smart and about to go out of her mind staying at home."

"What's the prognosis on your father?" Kennedy asked, changing the subject.

"He's getting stronger every day. It's my mother I'm more worried about. She's wearing herself out keeping vigil twenty-four-seven."

The media had been speculating like crazy. Word on the street was that the studio would be acquired. Kennedy had hoped and prayed that wasn't the case, and primarily for selfish reasons. She'd been promised a talk show, and although it was written in her contract, the possibility of such a thing materializing would be virtually nil if the studio had a change in management.

Perhaps she should talk to Salim about it. He was the one looking for new ideas and cutting-edge programming. But she didn't want to sound self-serving so she hesitated.

The doorbell rang, indicating their food had arrived. Soon after, Salim returned with a bag in hand. He refilled her wine and got a beer from the refrigerator.

"What's the first thing you'll do when you get to Yakima?" he asked, taking a slug from the bottle.

"Take a shower."

"You are kidding, aren't you?" His loud laughter made her laugh along with him. "I thought you'd be looking up old friends and going out to dinner."

"I'm working tomorrow. After a long drive, hooking up with friends is the last thing I'll do."

"But doesn't your mom live there? Aren't you going to see her?"

"I will eventually. My mother is still on honeymoon, husband number four," Kennedy added dryly.

"You don't sound very happy about it."

"I'm not. I've talked to the man on the phone and I'm

not impressed. She married him when I was in Japan so we never met."

"Sounds like she fell in love. How come you're not married?"

"How come you're not married?" she asked, turning the tables on him.

"I'm too busy and reluctant to settle down for a number of reasons."

"You sound like me."

"We're alike yet not alike," Salim said, leaning over and brushing his lips against hers. "Dammit, I can't seem to keep my hands off you."

She was having the same problem. Kennedy kissed him back, boldly, deepening the kiss and waiting for it to trigger the usual reaction.

Their tongues communed, melded and warred. Soon they were groping each other's most intimate parts. Kennedy's brain told her she should leave, but her limbs refused to cooperate. She was enjoying being with him and welcomed his touch.

He had her on her back, working her jacket off at the same time. Salim's free hand caressed a panty-hose-clad leg. "Take these off."

Sitting up, she quickly slipped them off, not caring if she got a run. His bunched muscles felt good under-hand and she inhaled the fresh scent of his body wash.

"Should we stop before this goes further?" he asked in a husky voice.

How could she answer that question when both her head and body wanted him to go on? It was wrong, even foolish of her to want to sleep with the man again. You didn't get involved with someone on the job, especially your boss. But she was beyond reasoning now.

Each time they'd been together was better and better. No other love affair compared to this. If they had no expectations beyond the time they'd spent together, well, why not?

Could she really handle it?

Kennedy tugged on the zipper of Salim's jeans. His erection sprang free, a hot, throbbing rod of steel in her palms. She closed her hands around him and began to slowly, rhythmically stroke. Strangled noises ripped from his throat, turning her on. She was already on fire and pulsating in places she didn't know pulsed. Her breasts felt swollen and heavy and ached for his touch.

Capturing his hand, she placed it on her breasts. The warmth and roughness of his palm turned her on even more. The friction his thumb created when he circled a nipple made her want to jump out of her skin. Kennedy grinded herself against him, liking the way his hard body felt against hers, liking his pulsing member against her core.

She was lost in the soapy smell of him, and wrapped in the warm seductive blanket that was the heat from his skin. Shifting her position, she bent her head, opened her mouth and took him in.

Salim was all hands now, his fingers probing. They settled in an area that was warm and moist. When he wiggled his fingers, she opened up and let him in. Flipping her onto her back, he straddled her. Kennedy, feeling his full erection, arched upward to take him in. He tugged off her panties before sliding out of his pants, then reached for her hand.

"Help me with this."

Where had the condom come from? Had he known this would happen? Had he guessed she wouldn't say no? Too late to think.

Inch by inch he found his way in. Kennedy's fingers raked his back. As they both moaned, the couch empathically groaned.

Kennedy enjoyed the full feeling of having him inside her. She loved that he nipped the sides of her neck. The slap-slapping of their bodies making contact was a seductive and heady turnon.

"Are you with me, baby?" Salim asked in his raspy voice.

"All the way."

She was right there with him, as she'd never been with a man before. She could so easily get used to this—to him.

With a final thrust her whole world exploded. Kennedy convulsed, shuddered and bit his lower lip. They hung on as his own climax took over.

The realization hit her hard. She'd fallen for a man

that she could never have. Their lifestyles, wants and needs would never mesh. Somewhere along the way the brick wall around her heart had come tumbling down.

She wanted this man as she'd never wanted anyone before and she was prepared to accept him just as he was.

Chapter 14

Shelli balanced baby Daniella on her hip as Kennedy pushed herself out from behind the wheel of the car. She took a moment to stretch before hugging her sister-in-law and niece.

"How was the drive, hon?" Shelli inquired, handing the baby to her.

"It was uneventful and long. The scenery is always lovely though."

Shelli picked up the small overnight bag Kennedy had set down.

"Just look at my beautiful girl," she cooed, kissing the baby's plump cheek. There was no sign of

Kennedy's brother, Lincoln, so after a minute or so she asked, "Where's my brother?"

"Working. Things have been tight financially and he's taken on a second job. You must be hungry," Shelli said, leading the way into the kitchen.

A delectable aroma came from the oven, making Kennedy realize how hungry she was. Shelli could have been a gourmet cook if she put her mind to it. She claimed cooking helped her relax.

Kennedy settled the baby on her lap and watched Shelli remove a container from the refrigerator. She poured them two glasses of sweet tea. When Kennedy shifted the baby into a more comfortable position, the slight movement made her realize that she was still sore from Salim's incredible lovemaking.

"What's going on with you, girl? How's the new job?" Shelli asked, stirring a pot on the stove.

Kennedy filled her in on what had been happening at the studio.

"It sounds like you have your hands full. What do you think will happen if the owner passes away?"

Kennedy huffed out a sigh. She didn't want to think about it or the possible loss of the show she'd been promised.

"The studio might be bought," she answered. "The son would much rather be doing something worthwhile in a Third World country and the daughter has two little girls. She may not have the time or the inclination to deal with the stress of managing a television studio."

"What does this mean for you if the place is sold?" Shelli asked, sipping on her iced tea and eyeing Kennedy over the rim of her glass.

"It was never meant to be a permanent job. I'm a consultant hired with the promise of a television show if I can whip the son into shape."

"And have you whipped him yet?"

Kennedy smiled wryly. "He's as whipped as he wants to be."

"I'm picking up more here than you're saying," Shelli said astutely. "You two are involved."

"Depends on how you define involved."

Shelli flung her arms around her, startling baby Daniella. The child began to cry. "This is so exciting. Since I've known you I don't recall you ever seriously dating anyone."

"I'm not dating," Kennedy said quickly.

"Then why does your face light up every time you talk about Salim?"

"You're imagining things."

"Hardly."

Shelli's comments were way off base and made Kennedy feel she must be transparent. Her sex life—or lack of one—was not something she wished to discuss with her sister-in-law.

"I hate to say this," she admitted, "but I'm not

finding the job challenging anymore. I much preferred the old Salim. Turning a free-spirited man into a buttoned-down executive will just suck the life out of him."

Shelli eyed her shrewdly. "What about your bonus? Put your emotions aside and think money, girl. Think of the television show you were promised."

"I am, but I'm also thinking how I can somehow manage to get in on these documentaries. There's got to be a way to make Salim's changes in programming work for me."

The doorbell rang and the conversation came to an abrupt end.

"I'm not expecting company," Shelli muttered, taking the baby back from Kennedy and hurrying off to answer.

She returned with her mother-in-law and a gaunt man who stood head and shoulders above Taiko.

"Look who's here to see you," Shelli said as they entered the kitchen.

Kennedy was swept into her mother's warm embrace and almost choked.

"You look wonderful," Taiko said, finally putting her away from her. "Being abroad agreed with you. You've lost weight and I like what you've done with your hair."

"Domo arigato," Thank you, Kennedy said in Japanese.

"Do itashi mashiti." You're very welcome came the automatic return.

Kennedy swept a handful of streaked hair off her face. It was the weekend and she'd lost the headband. The man standing next to her mother waited to be introduced.

"This is Jack," Taiko said, beaming up at her unsmiling spouse. "Jack, this is my daughter, Kennedy."

Her mother's husband nodded his greeting. "You're the one who went to Tokyo, right?"

"Yes, I did. Mom tells me you're just back from your Hawaii honeymoon. Was it your first time there?"

He nodded again.

"And what did you think?" she prodded.

"We have pictures," Taiko said, rifling through the hobo bag she was carrying. "That's if I can find them. Where's Linc?"

"Working," Shelli explained. "Let me put the little one down and we can have a glass of bubbly to celebrate you getting married and Kennedy's homecoming."

"I'd rather have a beer," Jack said ungraciously.

Kennedy bit her tongue. How did a sensible woman continue to pick losers like this man? Maybe her mother just didn't like being alone.

She went to the refrigerator and got her stepfather a Bud. By then Taiko had found her pictures. She set them on the table.

"Come see how much fun we had," she called.

Kennedy joined her mother and stepfather and began politely looking through the photographs. The couple had gotten married on the island and her mother looked radiant in a flowing white gown, her neck wreathed in leis. Her unsmiling husband chomped on a cigar beside her.

"Check this pic out," Jack said, handing Kennedy one from the pile.

Kennedy grimaced. Although her mother had maintained a very nice figure, she had no business in a thong. Kennedy suspected she'd been talked into wearing the getup by her husband.

She waited until Shelli had returned from putting the baby to bed to ask Jack the question that had been foremost on her mind. "What is it you do, Jack?"

He took a long pull on his beer and watched her carefully. "Oh, a little of this and a little of that."

Translation: he was unemployed. Her mother needed to have her head examined. Where had Linc and Roosevelt been when the freeloader came on the scene?

"Champagne?" Shelli asked quickly, removing a chilled bottle from the refrigerator and without getting an answer popped the cork.

A drink Kennedy could definitely use. She savored the bubbly and decided a change of topic might be in order.

"So is everyone looking forward to the family reunion?" she lied, making conversation.

"I'm not," Jack groaned.

Kennedy decided to ignore him.

"All your stepbrothers and sisters will be there," Taiko said excitedly. "Even some of my exes are planning on coming."

Kennedy's stomach did that bucking thing. She couldn't think of any of them she'd be excited to see. One in particular. She'd never been able to forgive him for taking advantage of an innocent child.

Shelli was now unloading food from the oven.

"I'll set the table," Kennedy offered. "Will Linc be home any time soon?" She hoped her brother would show up. It would make it that much easier to get through the meal.

"I'm hoping," his wife said, setting down a dish of corn bread next to the macaroni and cheese.

Halfway through the meal Taiko said something that got Kennedy's attention.

"I heard Marna and her buddy, Summer, are in town."

"Where did you hear this from?" Kennedy asked.

"In passing. A friend of Jack's mentioned she and the Alaskan boyfriend aren't getting along. She supposedly came home with him and then they split."

Kennedy looked at her mother expectantly. "Marna must be staying somewhere."

She shrugged before reluctantly saying, "I'll ask around."

"That *woman* ran off with Kennedy's money," Shelli muttered, sounding incensed. "She didn't deposit the money she was supposed to in their joint bank account, nor did she pay Kennedy's bills. Marna's irresponsible actions put Kennedy in debt. Tell them how your car was repossessed and how close you came to foreclosure. Someone like that shouldn't be allowed to get away with what she did. If I were Kennedy I'd have her arrested for theft."

A lively discussion followed. Lincoln showed up in the middle of it. Kennedy went through the motions of greeting her brother but she was already thinking ahead. Tomorrow she planned on finding Marna. She didn't expect to get her money back, but she needed some answers.

Salim placed the receiver back on its cradle. According to Nate things were going well in Cité Soleil, but they definitely could use a pair of extra hands.

In a fit of restlessness he crossed over to the window and looked out on the garden below. He'd always known he wasn't cut out to sit behind some desk stroking inflated egos and trying to convince people to see things his way. He should be there in Haiti doing work that mattered, and helping the locals get treatment that was very much needed.

He glanced at the clock on the wall realizing that if he didn't leave now, he would be late for his next appointment. The detective, Phillip Campbell, was waiting for him at a bar in Pike's Place Market. He'd called earlier indicating he had the detailed information Salim needed.

What was it Phillip had uncovered? Not that it would make much difference in how he felt about the woman. Physical attraction aside, there were many things about Kennedy that he'd come to like. She was loyal, dependable and excellent at assessing the root of a problem. Add to that being sexy as all hell.

Deciding to leave Deka parked in her usual spot, Salim walked the few blocks to Rachel's. The bar was named after the public market's bronze piggy bank located on the first level. It was a reasonably warm Friday evening and the streets were crowded with people on their way home to the suburbs.

Inside, the tavern was filled with more piggylike things. Salim wove his way around the happy hour crowd and headed for Phillip Campbell. The detective sat on a stool, his fingers drumming the manila folder occupying the seat next to him. He was the type of man who blended into a crowd easily; a good thing for a P.I.

"What are you drinking?" Salim asked, picking up the folder and sliding onto the stool.

"Whatever's on tap would be fine by me."

"Two Rainiers, please," Salim said, signaling to the bartender.

A couple of chilled mugs, the condensation still clinging to them, slid their way.

"Should I go ahead and open this?" Salim inquired, deciding, why prolong the suspense?

"It's ugly," Phillip warned.

Salim was already prepared for anything. Gritting his teeth, he removed several pieces of paper and read them before setting the file back on the bar.

"How did you get this information?" he asked, tight-lipped.

"Hospital records. I have a contact that's very good at ferreting out these things."

Salim's fingers drummed the wooden surface. Bile rose in his throat. If the man who'd violated Kennedy was anywhere around, he would have delighted in punching him in the face.

"What kind of monster would violate a ten-year-old girl?" he muttered aloud.

"The kind of monster that married the mother and then attempted to sue her for alimony. The second husband was a sick SOB. He forced himself on his stepdaughter on several occasions. Who knows how this would have ended if the brothers hadn't suspected and intervened? The oldest one almost killed him. I have the police report right here."

Salim was still reeling from what he'd learned. He'd heard a lot in his lifetime and even witnessed some horrible atrocities in the countries he'd visited, but when he'd started the investigation, this was the last thing he'd expected to uncover. It literally made him sick.

"And you've found no evidence that she was ever involved with my father?" he asked, trying to hold down the bile at the back of his throat.

"Nothing's surfaced that would lead me to believe she is," Phillip Campbell answered. "In fact I can't find evidence that's she's been involved with a man recently. What's the next step? Do you want me to keep digging?"

"No. I think I have enough," Salim said, snapping the folder shut. He was starting to feel slimy about invading Kennedy's privacy.

He was getting a better picture now, understanding Kennedy's need to maintain control and her wariness of men in general. She'd let her guard down, trusting him enough to sleep with him, and allowing him insight into the vulnerable lovely person she really was.

"This concludes our business," he said to Phillip. "Send me an invoice and I'll get a check out to you immediately."

The men shook hands.

"It's been a pleasure doing business with you," the detective said. "Call me if I can be of help in the future."

"I will. You've done a great job."

After the detective left, Salim sat at the bar replaying last evening's events. He'd seen the passionate side of Kennedy and he'd held her in his arms as if there was no tomorrow. And somewhere along the way, he'd fallen in love.

Given the kind of childhood she'd had, she deserved someone who loved her unconditionally and was in a position to care for her.

But he wasn't sure she was as interested in him as he was in her. In many ways they were two different people. Kennedy was conservative and liked things in order while he operated by the seat of his pants.

He missed her and needed to hear her voice. It could be the beer talking but, regardless, he needed to make contact.

Salim got out his cell phone and punched in Kennedy's number. His breath hitched as he waited for her to pick up.

Chapter 15

On the drive back to Seattle, Kennedy reflected on her weekend in Yakima. All things considered, it hadn't been bad. She'd had a nice visit with everyone.

After several hours of trying to find Marna, Kennedy had given up. Someone must have tipped off her cousin she was in town because she was nowhere to be found. Kennedy had gone to the address Jack claimed Marna was staying at only to be told her cousin was away for the weekend. She'd left a message asking for Marna to get in touch.

Kennedy turned on the radio and found a smooth jazz station. Humming along, she concentrated on the winding roads ahead. She'd been concerned about Jack, but her mother seemed happy with him, and it wasn't Kennedy's place to tell her she thought her husband was a waste of space. Instead they'd spent much of their time planning the upcoming family reunion.

Kennedy had decided to look at the gathering as an opportunity to put some demons to bed. If stepfather number two had the nerve to show up uninvited, she'd let him know exactly what she thought of him. It would be therapeutic and long overdue.

She was so deep in thought she almost missed hearing the ringing phone. Fumbling through her purse, she finally found it.

"Hello."

Salim's deep rumbling voice came at her. "Are you home yet?"

She clenched the steering wheel harder than she should and concentrated on the road. "No. I'm still driving."

"I was hoping we could talk."

What was so urgent that it couldn't wait until tomorrow when she was back at work? Maybe he wanted to make sure she didn't get the wrong idea about them sleeping together, not that she ever would. Someone like Salim Washington would not be interested in something long-term. Their personalities were too different and their aspirations like night and day.

Still something possessed her to say, "If you need to see me, I could swing by your place on my way home."

"Would you mind? It's not exactly business, we just need to get a couple of things straight," he answered, confirming her worst fears. "And this might be our only opportunity to have a one-on-one discussion without interruption."

Every stomach muscle clenched. At least after having this conversation she would know exactly where she stood.

For the next hour Kennedy conjured up the worst scenarios she could possibly think of. Maybe Salim would use his father's illness as an excuse to sever their business relationship. She had a contract, but there was nothing to stop him from breaking it, even though he was still required to pay her. Maybe he regretted crossing the line with her. Anyone with a smidgen of common sense knew business and pleasure just didn't mix. She'd already broken one of her own cardinal rules: never get involved with the boss.

There was no point in making herself crazy, she was almost at his home and would soon find out. Kennedy circled the block, finally finding a place to park. At Salim's door she took a deep breath and wiped her sweaty palms on her jeans.

Before she could press the buzzer the door flew open.

"How was the drive?" Salim asked, standing aside so she could enter.

"Uneventful." She wasn't about to share with him

the anxiety attack she'd just staved off, nor did he need to know that her pulse was racing way out of control.

"You look like you could use a cup of tea. Or would you prefer a cool drink?"

"Tea please," she said, following him into his kitchen and taking a seat at the table.

Salim seemed calm, cool, collected and certainly more together than she. He was the one in charge now. He made the tea and handed her a cup.

"What did you want to talk to me about?" Kennedy asked, getting to the point. The suspense was killing her.

"Oh, that. I wanted to discuss what's happening between us." He sounded so matter-of-fact. Here it came.

Oblivious of the heat from the mug, Kennedy waited for him to go on. When he didn't she said, "You're going to apologize and tell me it should never have happened?"

"No apology necessary, at least not from me."

Feeling far too vulnerable, she nibbled on her lower lip and waited.

"I'm sorry for thinking that you were having an affair with my old man way back then. I was wrong," he apologized.

He could have knocked her over with a feather. This was why he had wanted to see her? She had not been expecting this. Salim humbling himself?

"What made you change your mind about me?" she ventured.

"I got to know you. I like you. I think I misjudged you."

Her feelings for him went way beyond like. There was more to it than him having a change of mind. She sensed it.

"Apology accepted," she said, taking a small sip of her tea and letting it settle. She was beginning to have feelings for him and he was talking about liking her. Was this as romantic as it got?

Salim's fingers caressed the nape of her neck and massaged the supple flesh. Kennedy relaxed, enjoying the heat from his hands.

"That feels good," she said, rotating her neck.

Salim's hands moved downward, kneading her shoulders. She leaned into him practically purring. He kissed the skin behind her ear and began nibbling on her lobe. Like a cat in full heat, Kennedy arched her back.

"You've got some tension right here," Salim said, his thumb manipulating a particularly tight spot. "And here."

It had been a tense weekend. She'd been so on guard and so concerned for her mother, worried to death she'd made another mistake, marrying yet another loser. Finding out that Marna, the source of her problems, was back in town hadn't been easy, either. Kennedy had geared herself up for a confrontation that hadn't materialized. And now she was trying to sort out her feelings for a man that was unattainable. It all seemed too much.

"We should sit on the sofa and get more comfortable," Salim suggested.

What she should do was head home to the relative comfort of her own house where she could have space and think this through. But of course she ignored the little voice whispering in her ear and followed him out into the living room.

"So, tell me about your weekend," Salim said when they were seated and he continued to massage her tense shoulders. "Did you have a fun visit with your mother and brother?"

Kennedy gave the expected answer. "I enjoyed seeing them again. Time goes way too fast. How was your weekend?"

He filled her in, telling her all about how he'd played basketball with some buddies and that he'd been in touch with his partner, Nate.

"My sister is coming into the studio tomorrow."

Salim's fingers were now kneading her lower back, and purring noises came from the back of her throat.

"She's very practical and business minded, and far better suited to running a studio. I'm hoping she'll step in and take over for me. Of course there's the issue of Leonard, as well. He's not going to be happy with a corporate wife."

Kennedy thought it best to keep her opinion to herself. Salim's hands were now under her T-shirt and his fingers were exploring her flesh. His touch flooded her with such longing she could barely keep her hands to herself. When his tongue flicked the sides of her neck and he began nipping, she clung to him. Salim's hands were now on her lace-clad breasts. His fingers stroking her nipples set off a reaction that began at her core. She moaned and let him pull her onto his lap.

Through the denim of her jeans she could feel his hardness. No denying the physical attraction between them, but she wanted so much more. She didn't just want to be some guy's plaything. She'd been there and done that. A child didn't know better.

It was only through years of therapy that she'd come to understand that love didn't necessarily mean having a man remove your clothing and touch you in intimate places. Love was a mind thing, a connection that couldn't be explained.

Salim was now sliding her blouse over her head. He ran a finger across her exposed flesh right above where the lace of the bra plunged. Kennedy reached for the buttons on his shirt and slid her hands through the fuzz on his chest. She laid her head against the broad expanse of hardness and inhaled the fresh, soapy smell of him.

When Salim began a slow, rhythmic stroking of her breasts, all the tension from the tough weekend disappeared. She was literally putty in his hands and she was enjoying every single minute of being malleable.

"We should take this to the bedroom," Salim suggested in a voice heavily laced with sex. He didn't wait for her answer but brought her slowly to her feet.

His bedroom was by far the largest room in the house. Flipping off the light, he pulled down shades the same hunter-green color as the exterior shutters before leading her toward the gigantic bed.

Salim took off his jeans while she stripped off the rest of her clothes. His erection was a magnificent thing and a definite sign that she excited him. She no longer thought about where this might or might not go. She just went with her feelings.

Kennedy wrapped a palm around his shaft and squeezed gently. She used the pad of her thumb to slowly circle the tip of his member.

Salim's long, low moan and probing fingers made her squirm. She angled herself so that his fingers reached deep inside her. The strangled sounds now coming from the back of her throat excited them both. His thumping erection pressed into her stomach. He was alive and pulsating, beating a rapid tattoo against her flesh. She wanted him deep inside her and would do just about anything to have him there.

When Salim flicked his tongue across her hardened nipples, Kennedy clutched his back and moaned.

"Yes, baby, yes," he said, grabbing her buttocks and bringing her up hard against him.

Kennedy's breasts felt heavy and full. In a wanton act, she offered her nipples up to him. But instead of taking them into his mouth, Salim rubbed the wiry hairs of his chest against the hardened nubs, driving her wild with the friction. He paused just long enough to open a drawer on the nightstand and find a foil-covered package.

By the time they'd climbed onto his Cadillac of a bed she was experiencing a severe case of separation anxiety. He handed her the foil package and Kennedy used her mouth to help him shield himself. He suckled on her fingers, taking them slowly into his mouth. Knuckle by knuckle he made love to each one. If he made love like this—slow, easy, sensually—she would be completely his.

When she arched into him Salim's skin felt hot, slick and inviting. She relished the heat coming off him, liking the slight sheen on his skin, and savoring the salty taste of his flesh that she peppered with kisses.

Salim grinded into her, then nestled between her thighs. She could feel how excited he was. Kennedy let the tip of his shaft settle against the curls at her apex. When he probed for entrance, she adjusted her position slightly, taking him in one slow ecstatic inch at a time.

Kennedy's fingers raked his back as their movements synchronized. A slow crescendo began to build and then finally a tidal wave. Salim took her to places she'd never visited before until it ended in a colorful and beautiful explosion. It would be something she'd remember for years.

With the return of reality, Kennedy's common sense kicked in. She and Salim were two people living in the moment and enjoying what each had to offer. They had no place to go beyond the here and now.

Could she continue living in the moment and want nothing more?

"Hi, Kennedy. Good to see you again, especially under better circumstances," Christiane said, sticking her head into Kennedy's office the next day. "Diane said you would be a good person to get to know."

Kennedy liked Salim's sister instinctively.

"Come in," she invited, patting the chair across from her. "How's your first day so far?"

The resemblance between brother and sister was uncanny. Christiane was the female version of Salim, a striking woman with light eyes and the same chiseled features as her brother. She was smartly dressed in a red trapeze jacket and black slacks and didn't look anything at all like the typical, harried mother.

Crossing one leg over the other, she propped a hand under her chin and stared Kennedy in the eye.

"Diane tells me you were hired to mentor my brother," she said. "That's got to be a huge challenge."

Since she wasn't sure where this was going, Kennedy chose her words carefully. "I'm a consultant hired by your father to work with Salim. I'm to get him up to speed to take over the role of president."

"Hmmm. That's interesting especially since my brother has no interest in running a studio."

"Really?" Kennedy responded, her loyalty kicking in. She made sure to keep her expression neutral. "Salim's doing a great job as company president."

"I'm sure he is. What's this about him wanting to introduce documentaries to prime time? I hear the team is dead set against it but he's determined to push ahead?"

Kennedy could only imagine what else she'd heard. Leonard, her husband, was the one most violently opposed.

"Why don't you ask Salim about his plans for the studio?" Kennedy said diplomatically.

"Actually, I wanted to get your take on it first. Leonard's been ranting and raving, claiming my brother's making a huge mess of things. He thinks you should be doing a better job of reining him in."

"Me?" Kennedy's eyebrows rose. She was not about to touch that comment with a hundred-foot pole. It was much safer to take the conversation in an entirely different direction. "Salim did say you'd be coming into the studio to learn the business from the ground up. If I can help in any way I'd be glad to."

"I'll take you up on that offer," Christiane said, her eyes sparkling, teasingly. "Make me your pet project. It's time TSW had a female at the helm."

"That would be awesome," Kennedy said, smiling

ruefully and thinking how the stuffy execs would react to a woman in charge.

She was also smart enough to know that she needed someone influential in her corner. Christiane Green could make a good ally and Kennedy needed a friend.

Chapter 16

"There is no way I am going to sit here and watch you run this company into the ground," Leonard said, stabbing a finger inches from Salim's nose.

Salim slapped closed the folder he'd been browsing through. He'd been reading Phillip Campbell's report from cover to cover, and piecing together Kennedy's life. The more he read about her upbringing, the more it made him angry. His feelings for Kennedy were well beyond the admiration stage by now. He would gladly have snapped the neck of the man who'd violated her.

He stood and crossed his arms under his armpits.

"Back off, Leonard," he said rudely. "I've made my decision. I will not renew David McFarland's contract and that's that. He's costing the studio plenty and at this point he's more a liability than an asset. The man's a loose cannon with a substance abuse problem. TSW's paid out huge sums to keep his mishaps under wraps. Enough is enough."

"Have you lost your mind? David McFarland pulls in viewers. He's smoking hot," Leonard shouted back. "It's in TSW's best interest to keep him." Realizing he might have crossed the line, Leonard lowered his voice. "Look, I know you don't want to be here. You know you don't want to be here. So why don't you just let me make the decisions and everything will continue to run just fine."

"Forget about it, Leonard. I like making decisions that move this company forward. It's been stagnant for far too long. TSW needs to join the twenty-first century. One of my first priorities is trimming the fat." He eyeballed Leonard, gauging his reaction.

"There is no fat," Leonard sputtered in his usually arrogant way. "This studio has been lean and mean for several years. Before you make any drastic changes, you need to run them by seasoned veterans. You could learn a thing or two from us." He puffed out his chest.

Salim had had enough of his brother-in-law. He drew himself up to his full height and faced Leonard. "I've never pulled rank with you before but I'm doing so now. As the president of TSW I have an obligation to ensure that this studio remains in the black. The money we spend on bottled water alone could feed an entire orphanage for a year. There are people on the payroll I know nothing about much less what they do."

"That's why we have accountants. In your role, you aren't expected to know everyone. On an entirely different note, I wish you'd talk sense into your sister."

"My sister is very sensible."

"Not lately. She has two children that need her. She has no business here."

"As I recall they're school-aged children. Christiane has always been the kind of woman who needs to use her brain."

Leonard snorted. "I should have known you'd encourage her in this nonsense. My wife should be home raising her kids and taking care of me, not wasting her time playing businesswoman."

Salim's brother-in-law was really pissing him off now. How his sister put up with him was way beyond Salim's comprehension.

"Christiane was gainfully employed when you first met her," Salim reminded Leonard. "To sell high-end real estate you need to be a lot more than decorative."

"All of her referrals were from family and friends. That doesn't require a whole lot of business acumen," Leonard jabbed, putting down his wife.

"Regardless of what you think, she made a decent living. There are many transferable skill sets in that line of work. Diplomacy and the ability to deal with challenging people are needed. You have to be fairly versatile to crunch numbers, drop everything when a client calls and find them that dream house."

Leonard made a huge production of looking at his watch. He cleared his throat. "We're late. We're supposed to be meeting in the viewing room to look at those documentaries you're considering buying."

Salim looked at the wall clock. They were almost a half hour behind schedule. "You're right. Time tends to get away from us in this business. Let's go."

He headed out with a reluctant, resentful Leonard trailing behind him.

Where on earth was Salim? He was late and the executive team was already talking about leaving. Most shifted restlessly in their seats. There had been loud mutterings about having more important things to do. Some were already standing and having hushed conversations with each other.

Four documentaries had been selected for viewing. The idea was to decide which TSW might be interested in acquiring the distribution rights to, and which would most pique the audience's interest.

Kennedy had made several excuses for Salim's tardiness. She was fresh out of them now.

"Leonard's not here, either," Mark Wallingford said, sliding up next to her. "He's always punctual."

"Leonard and Salim may be meeting," Kennedy answered easily. "I'll buzz Diane to see what's going on."

But Diane wasn't answering her phone and neither was Salim.

"I'll go and see what the holdup is," Kennedy volunteered. "Perhaps we should start without him."

Kennedy hurried off hoping that by the time she returned Mark would have made an executive decision to start running the film.

Diane wasn't sitting at her desk when Kennedy entered the outer room. She poked her head in his office, spotted his appointment book lying wide open and checked to see if he'd been double-booked. He'd penciled in the documentary viewing so it wasn't as if he'd forgotten. Maybe he was on his way.

That same manila folder with her name written on it caught Kennedy's eye. She noted the personal and confidential sticker and because it lay wide open she couldn't resist.

She darted a furtive glance at the outer room to make sure Diane hadn't returned before glancing at the first document within her reach. Initially she'd thought it might be her personnel file with the results of the background and drug tests TSW had insisted on. But it was a report of another kind.

She noticed the man's signature at the bottom: why did the name Phillip Campbell keep popping up? Kennedy darted a second look outside. She'd hate to be caught snooping, but this was important. She scrutinized the remaining papers carefully, getting angrier and angrier. There were details and dates about her life on display, things she'd never told another living soul.

She shuffled through the remaining papers quickly, confirming that the information was all about her. Then, spotting an invoice, she examined it carefully. The name of the detective agency was very prominent— Campbell, P.I., Services for Hire. It had cost Salim a bundle to investigate her.

Closing the folder, she raced from his office and waited until she got to the hallway to gulp air. Kennedy braced herself against the wall and waited for the ceiling to stop folding and unfolding like an accordion. She was furious now, way beyond angry.

How dare Salim investigate her? He'd betrayed her and used her in a very cavalier way; making love to her and pretending that he cared when in fact it was an act. Deep down he still believed she was involved with his father. She was even angrier with herself for falling for a man who didn't trust her. She needed to get over it and move on pronto.

It irked Kennedy that Salim had been happy to take what she had to offer and, without the slightest twinge of conscience, use her. How could a man who made love to her be so two-faced? He'd uncovered things about her he had no business knowing and weren't at all relevant to her position here. God, she was mad!

Kennedy gulped in another mouthful of air. She

needed to calm down and get back to the viewing room. She'd figure out how to deal with this later.

There was a definite set to her jaw when she retraced her steps. She entered a darkroom to find the film already running and took a seat determined to concentrate.

For the next two hours she watched mindlessly as the camera followed two people with full-blown AIDS, chronicling their friends' and families' handling of the situation. She witnessed children maimed and blinded in India so that they could become professional beggars and help their parents, and she almost lost it watching genital mutilation of prepubescent children.

Finally it was over with. When the lights flickered on, the silence seemed to go on forever. Then suddenly everyone began talking in a rush.

"Brilliant!" someone shouted. "Utterly brilliant."

"That last director is a genius."

"Now, that I would buy."

The last documentary had been so moving and powerful it left the viewers with an indelible impression. It also served to take Kennedy's mind off her own issues, at least temporarily. She was still angry at Salim, but less apt to confront him until she'd thought about it some more.

Kennedy didn't realize that Christiane Green had been a part of the viewing audience until the woman stopped her on the way out.

"I should have saved you a seat," Salim's sister greeted her.

Kennedy smiled widely at the woman. "Now, that would have been nice. What did you think about the lineup?"

"I loved it. Although love is probably too strong a word, given the sobering nature of the subjects."

"Films like that are designed to get people sitting up and thinking. They were brilliant choices. Your brother may be onto something."

"It's a pretty honest depiction of life outside the United States," Salim interjected, coming up behind them. He linked an arm through the women's. "How are my two favorite girls?"

Kennedy could barely look at him. How could she pretend to joke with a man who hired a P.I. to go digging into her life? He'd blindsided her by being unethical and underhanded. He'd never struck her as the devious type. And yet the evidence of his deception sat on his desk in an open folder.

"We are not girls," Christiane said, straightening him out. "How would you like it if we referred to you as a boy?"

"Hey, at the ripe old age of thirty-three, I'd be thrilled."

"Well, we're not thrilled. Ever heard of the women's movement?"

"Salim, those were three of the most moving documentaries I've ever seen," Yolanda Smythe, the female executive, said, coming up to them. She turned her brilliant smile on Christiane. "You're Salim's sister, aren't you? You look so much alike."

Christiane nodded and held out her hand.

"I'm Yolanda Smythe," she said, wrapping a hand around Christiane's. "I heard something about you coming on board."

"I hope what you heard was good."

Yolanda smiled and bobbed her head. "I'm just glad to have another smart female on my side. You'll soon find out this is a very male-dominated world."

Salim was now surrounded by several of the executives. Leonard Green came out of nowhere, placing a possessive hand on his wife's upper arm.

"We need to talk," he hissed.

"We can do that when we get home," she hissed right back. "Now is not the appropriate time or place."

Kennedy loved it that Christiane stood up for herself. Leonard was a controlling, domineering bully and would easily run you over if you allowed him to.

"I think it is," Leonard insisted.

Preferring not to be privy to the uncomfortable exchange, Yolanda and Kennedy kept walking.

"I've been meaning to ask you to lunch," Yolanda surprised Kennedy by saying. "It looks like our boss is going to be tied up for a bit, so how about we grab a cup of coffee in the commissary?"

"I'd like that."

Privately, Kennedy thought Yolanda Smythe was the savviest and possibly brightest member of the executive team. As the sole woman in a male-dominated environment, she'd done her best to fit in. Kennedy also suspected she was carrying a major torch for Salim. She was curious to find out what Yolanda wanted with her.

On their way they ran into Charissa, the starlet whose last name seemed to evade everyone. The diva had a cell phone pressed to her ear. She nodded in their direction before floating off.

"Beautiful woman," Kennedy said, making conversation and waiting to see how Yolanda would segue into her conversation.

"Charissa is difficult as all hell. That woman is the ultimate drama queen. She's mastered the art of the tantrum."

They'd reached the commissary. Midafternoon meant it was fairly deserted and you had your choice of seats. After grabbing coffee, Yolanda led them to a nook at the back of the room.

"I've been curious about you," she began. "I mean you arrived out of nowhere. The entire management team wondered about you."

"Why is that?" Kennedy asked, carefully.

"You're beautiful, polished and from what I hear, speak several languages. Everyone's awed because you're classy, well educated and you've got great manners. Most think you've been stuck with the awful job of trying to change a man who doesn't want to be changed." She shook her head. "I must sound disloyal."

"Not at all. It's my job to bring out the best in people and Salim wasn't at all difficult to work with," she lied.

Yolanda took a sip of her coffee. Her brown eyes sparkled challengingly. "You're telling me it wasn't tough getting Salim to change?"

"Not at all. He's been great."

"He's headstrong and opinionated."

"I've found him to be very fair and open-minded."

"You must have the hots for him," Yolanda said, eyeing Kennedy over her cup.

"Who doesn't?" Kennedy threw back.

Yolanda's hearty laughter rang out. "Girlfriend, you are funny. Salim would be perfect for a one-night hookup. He's got about the best body of anyone I know, but beyond that no. When I'm looking for a relationship it would be with an entirely different type."

"They don't come much better."

"I'm more into the buttoned-down type. Call me materialistic, but I want the four-thousand-square-foot house, the two luxury vehicles in the garage, the housekeeper and gardener."

"Salim's not exactly hurting," Kennedy came back. "I'd imagine if he were so inclined, he could provide you with what you want quite easily. He stands to inherit all this and he does have a trust fund."

"But that's the point, he doesn't really care about money and I do. I've worked really hard in a tough, male-oriented environment to get here. I have no interest in being squired around in a beat-up old pickup truck by a man who spends more time out of the country than in. I like being on the cocktail circuit and attending various social functions."

As angry as she was with Salim, Kennedy was not particularly comfortable with where the conversation was heading. She'd admired Yolanda and the way she handled herself professionally, but the executive was crossing a line and she wasn't going there with her.

"How did you get into the television business?" Kennedy asked, subtly changing the subject.

"I was a journalism major with grandiose ideas of wanting to be an anchor for one of the major players. One summer I interned as a production assistant and fell in love with the world of moviemaking."

"And the rest, as they say, is history. Look at you now. You've come a long way."

"Yes, I've risen rather quickly. Right after college I got hired on as a floor manager at the same studio where I'd interned. When I felt I had enough experience under my belt, I applied at TSW. I wanted to work for a black-owned company."

"And five years later you're the Program Marketing vice president and living your dream."

Yolanda leaned in as if she were confiding to her best

friend. "Some might say so, but I have other aspirations."

Curiosity prompted Kennedy to ask, "What are they?"

Kennedy suspected she was being told this for a reason. Yolanda probably hoped she would repeat it in the right ear. Salim's ear.

"Actually my goal is to be president of my own studio one day," the executive said.

Kennedy didn't miss a beat. "In that case, maybe you should be mentoring Salim or even Christiane. You could show them both the ins and outs of the biz. I know very little about the industry myself."

"So that's why Leonard's wife's been showing up," Yolanda said, pursing her lips. "I wondered why the sudden interest. I thought perhaps the kids were preparing themselves for Tanner passing over. Everyone's worried about the studio being sold."

Kennedy drained her cup and tuned in more sharply to the conversation. She'd never been a gossip, but at times it paid to keep an ear to the ground.

"I haven't heard a thing other than what I read in the paper," Kennedy said diplomatically. "Now, if you'll excuse me, I should be getting back. Can I mention to Christiane that you'd be interested in helping her learn the ropes?"

"Of course."

Leaving the woman sitting there, Kennedy decided

rather than go directly back to her office she'd go for a walk. The fresh air would give her time to figure out how to approach Salim. She was still feeling violated and resented her privacy being invaded.

Blue skies and sunlight, just what she needed. Kennedy shrugged out of the jacket covering her proper cap-sleeved shirt with the bow at the neck. She circled the parklike grounds several times, thinking. God, she was angry.

The ringing phone brought reality back home.

"This is Kennedy."

"Where are you?" Salim asked.

Determined to keep her voice neutral, she took a deep breath. "I had coffee with Yolanda and, rather than have lunch, decided to take a walk."

"Are you on the property?"

"Yes, I'm walking around the gardens."

"I'll be right out to join you."

Having him there was the last thing she needed.

Chapter 17

Mark walked into Salim's office just as he was heading out.

"Can I talk to you for a moment?" he asked.

"Can it wait? I should be free in an hour."

Salim had an inkling as to what it was about. Mark wanted to nail down the lineup for next season's shows. They'd discussed with the attorneys how to buy some of the leads out of their current contracts so they could introduce new blood.

"Having a meeting without me?" Leonard asked, sticking his head into Salim's office.

"We were just about to wrap up," Mark diplomatically responded. "What did you think of the films?"

"Depressing."

"Really?" Salim said.

"It's going to be a hard sell at prime time," Leonard muttered, shrugging his shoulders.

It would be a waste of breath to get him to change his mind. He was hell-bent on serving up the usual formula.

"Let's set up a meeting with our lawyers and hear their take about canceling our snoozers. I stay firm on buying some of these folks out of their contracts and letting them move on."

"Tell me you're not still thinking of terminating David McFarland? That would be the kiss of death to this studio," Leonard said rudely.

"Personally I think he's way overpaid and we would do well to separate ourselves from him," Salim said. "You did see the Sunday paper? He's fallen off the wagon and now he has another DUI."

"At least he's not like Charissa with a list of demands a mile long."

"Let's save this discussion for later," Mark proposed. "Salim has another appointment."

Leonard was still grumbling loudly as Salim grabbed his jacket.

"What about that agreement your father made with your assistant or whatever she is?" he said snidely.

"Does Tanner have an agreement with Diane?" Salim countered with a straight face.

"I was talking about the leadership coach, the

woman who shadows you. Your father promised her a bonus."

That stopped Salim in his tracks. "What bonus?"

"Tanner promised she'd have her own talk show."

The back of Salim's eyeballs burned. His old man would never promise such a thing unless he was getting something back in return.

"Kennedy's not a celebrity," he muttered. "I have to go. We'll talk about this later."

Leonard followed him down the hall while Mark headed off in the opposite direction.

"Come on, Salim, you had to know that there was something else in it for Kennedy or why would she still be here?"

Salim hustled off without another word. He didn't trust himself to be anywhere close to Leonard. He was now grappling with the fact that he was "business." And to think he was just a step away from falling hard for the woman.

Salim caught up with Kennedy as she paused to examine a budding shrub.

"Hey," he forced himself to say, "I had no idea you walked during lunch or I would have joined you."

She turned, and her eyes were colder than diamond chips as they flickered over him. "That's a surprise. I thought you knew everything there was to know about me."

He fell in step with her. "Are you upset with me for some reason?"

Kennedy didn't answer right off. It didn't take a rocket scientist to figure out she was angry. Well, he wasn't happy with her, either.

"I resent you invading my privacy," she snapped.

"How so?"

"You had me investigated! You hired a private eye to poke into my affairs! Nothing gives you the right to do that!"

His eyes narrowed. Phillip Campbell had assured him he was discreet and totally confidential. How had Kennedy found out what he'd been up to?

The best defense was usually an offense. "You were snooping, then?"

"Not snooping. You had a folder on your desk with my name on it. You left it wide open."

"If you looked at it, then you were snooping," he said.

"I'd call it finding out what I needed to know."

He placed a hand on her arm and she recoiled.

"Come on, Kennedy. I needed to know if you were the real deal or not. Can you blame me?"

"And what did you find out?"

"Nothing to support my initial suspicions."

Her icy laughter rang out. "Now, imagine that."

"If you're expecting apologies it's not going to happen. I was trying to protect my mother."

"It doesn't matter what your reasons were," she said, continuing to walk. "The fact that you were heartless enough to sleep with a woman you didn't trust says it all."

The business of the bonus still bothered him.

"What does sleeping with you have to do with any of this?" Salim shouted after her. "It's not like you didn't have your own agenda."

She cast narrowed eyes over her shoulder. "You don't get it, do you? I can't work for a person who doesn't trust me."

"Don't be ridiculous. You're making this bigger than it needs to be."

"I'm out of here! I quit! I'll let Diane know which address to forward my check to."

He'd been expecting excuses and denials, not this. Given what he'd learned about Kennedy, he didn't think she could afford to quit.

"Come on, Kennedy. Be reasonable. Be professional," Salim cajoled. "There's a bonus at stake here. Didn't my old man promise you your own show? That's reason enough to stick around."

"No, it's not, especially if I have to work with you." Not giving him a second glance, Kennedy left.

He didn't follow her because he knew it would be pointless. He'd made a huge mess of things.

It would be wiser to let Kennedy have her space. He needed time himself to figure out what he could do to recover. He'd fallen in love with the woman, but would love be enough?

* * *

"Is everything okay?" Diane asked in her usual no-nonsense manner as Kennedy strode by.

Kennedy balanced the carton holding the few personal items she'd brought into the studio on her hip, and gave Tanner's executive assistant a wan smile.

"I'm taking these things to the car. Today is my last day."

Di removed her glasses and set them on the desk in front of her. "Did I miss something?"

"No. I can't do it anymore. Call me at home if you have questions about anything at all. You have my number."

"What's going on?" Christiane asked, interrupting them. "Salim and I were just in a meeting. I asked what I thought was a perfectly reasonable question, and he almost bit my head off. Where are you going with that box?"

"Home."

Christiane's forehead wrinkled. "Did you and my idiot brother have a disagreement?"

Kennedy couldn't help the snort that came out.

"If you'll walk with me to the parking lot, I'll fill you in," she said.

Carrying the carton in her hand, Kennedy started off.

Christiane waited until they were outside to resume the conversation.

"Salim, much as I love him, can be a real jerk at times," she admitted. "He'll apologize eventually."

"I'll need more than an apology to get over what he did to me," Kennedy grumbled.

"It was that bad? Want me to beat him up for you?" Christiane put up her dukes. Her accompanying facial expression actually made Kennedy smile.

"I'd be happy if you could convince him to stay out of my personal affairs."

Kennedy shoved the carton and its contents in the trunk of the Lexus while Christiane watched.

The full impact of what she'd done finally hit her. This wasn't her car and perhaps her decision to quit was too impulsive. She would be back to square one with no means of transportation. She'd have to take out a loan to buy a car, providing someone would finance her.

Using the remote key, she opened the vehicle's doors and turned back to Christiane. "Let your brother know I'll return the company car next week. He can prorate the insurance and send me a bill."

Christiane grabbed Kennedy's wrists, forcing her to look at her. "I don't know what happened between the two of you, nor am I asking you to divulge, but my brother needs you. I've watched him change. He's become a man and he's so much happier and better adjusted for it. I credit that all to you."

Kennedy forced a smile. She wasn't mad at the woman. It was her brother she despised.

"That's about the nicest thing anyone has said to me in a long time. Thank you," she said sincerely. "Your brother hired a P.I. to investigate me. I'll never forgive him for that."

Christiane kept her voice low as she came closer. "Whether the idiot knows it or not, he's in love with you."

"That's ridiculous," Kennedy sputtered.

"And you're perfect for each other."

"I have to go," Kennedy said, the tears at the back of her throat almost choking her. She hopped into the car, and with a wave of her hand, took off. As she drove she had the most horrifying thought, what if Salim had slept with her because he thought she was easy? He'd accused her of having an affair with his father and he'd uncovered her deep, dark secret. He knew she'd been sexually abused at an early age. What if he thought she'd led her stepfather on?

Regardless, she'd let her emotions guide her. No one in their right mind quit a job before finding another. No one.

When someone knocked on his closed office door, Salim was fully expecting to find a repentant Kennedy on the other side.

"Come in," he shouted, wondering why Diane wasn't doing her usual efficient job of keeping drop-ins out.

His sister planted herself in front of his desk and folded her arms. "What a jerk you are."

"I love you, too."

"You just let the best thing that happened to you walk out your front door, and here you are seated behind a desk letting your pride get in the way."

Salim tossed down his pen. "Okay, speak to me in English. What are we talking about?"

"I just walked Kennedy to her car."

"She came whining to you."

Christiane folded her arms. "Actually no, she was pretty damn gracious considering everything you put her through. If you'd had me investigated you would be wearing your size-twelve shoe up your own hindquarters. You owe Kennedy an apology."

Despite his feeling low, Christiane's blunt comment made him smile. His sister seldom pulled punches and that's probably the only reason she and Leonard were still married.

"Apology for what? When I first met the woman it seemed obvious she was having an affair with our father. I mean why else would he hire her?"

"You really are an ass," Christiane snorted, shaking her head. "Kennedy was hired to groom you because our father realized he might not be around forever. He wanted to make sure that the studio remained in the family, and since you're male, then you obviously knew what you were doing. He clearly didn't think I could handle the role. Let's give Kennedy some credit for doing an awesome job with you."

"If I were promised my own show I'd do a bang-up job, as well," Salim muttered under his breath.

"Why does it bother you that Dad offered Kennedy her own program?"

He'd expected his sister to be stunned, even furious, but she didn't seem to care; maybe she didn't understand.

"Tanner's a smart businessman. There had to be something in it for him or he would never have offered Kennedy that kind of bonus."

Christiane perched on the edge of his desk, staring at him for a long time. "You are such a bozo," she said after a while. "What was in it for Dad was seeing you head up the company he built. He's wanted you involved in the business his whole life. What's eating you up right now is that you're in love with a woman you can't control, and angry at yourself for having fallen for her. Get over it."

"You're talking nonsense," Salim said, tight-lipped. "I'm furious that I was bulldozed into taking this position when frankly you'd do a better job. I'm not cut out for this industry and I have no patience with multiple personalities."

"You've done a great job in Dad's absence. I've heard him say numerous times how proud he is of you. Why haven't you been by to see him?"

Salim was completely taken aback. The old man had not exactly been generous with his compliments. But he should have known he would be keeping tabs on him. "I thought he wasn't supposed to have visitors."

"Family aren't exactly considered visitors," Christiane said, not cutting him any slack. "The man has survived several heart attacks and now he's undergoing another surgery in a couple of weeks. Can't you just let go of your anger and be supportive?"

Salim dug the tips of his fingers into his palms so hard it hurt. "It's not easy to forget what an SOB he was to our mother all these years."

"She got over it and so should you. Don't try to avoid the subject of Kennedy."

"I'm not."

"Yes, you are. What are you going to do about her?"

"Nothing. Absolutely nothing."

"That's plain dumb."

Salim's shrug infuriated her even more.

"I'm taking some time off and going to Haiti, and I'm leaving you to run the show."

"You're running away from responsibility as you typically do," Christiane snapped back. She placed her hands on her hips. "Leonard will gladly step up to the task and put his twelve cents in, especially if he thinks he's in charge."

Christiane would not let him make decisions that would negatively affect the business. There was some small comfort in knowing that. He could take two weeks off to get his head straight.

And do something meaningful and worthwhile.

Chapter 18

Salim shaded his eyes and tried to avoid squinting into the sun.

"Man, this heat is brutal," he said to his partner, Nate.

"You're getting soft," Nate shot back. "Must be all the sitting and shuffling papers at that desk job."

Salim's raw oath resounded. "Look who's talking, the man who's waffling about helping me at the airport tomorrow."

He turned his attention back to the crate he was having difficulty prying open. It was filled with supplies flown in from the States. The mindless work of opening up boxes and crates helped take his mind off Kennedy.

Nate paused for a moment to wipe his forehead on his shirtsleeve. He took a gulp of water and recapped the bottle.

"What we really need is a local in our corner, someone with pull so that we don't have to run back and forth hassling with customs to get medical equipment and medicine through."

"Know anyone?" Salim asked.

Nate had spent enough time in Haiti to make some valuable connections. He was good at striking up conversations with people he didn't know.

"Many of our volunteers are well connected. We should take advantage of their contacts. One is the prime minister's nephew."

"Good to know. Maybe he can do something about the supplies that sit at customs for weeks."

Nate nodded in agreement. "Maybe we'll get lucky networking at the prime minister's cocktail hour later. I say we put in another half hour before knocking off. The festival should still be going on then."

Salim had totally forgotten about the party, which really was a command performance. The foundation was going to be publicly recognized for its contributions to the AIDS fight. The event was actually a fundraiser with ridiculously high-priced tickets for sale.

This would be Salim's first social event since arriving in Haiti. From day one it had been work and more work. But he was slowly starting to feel more like his old self and he loved the feeling of accomplishment and the adrenaline rush.

Even his energy level was up and it had nothing to do with living a luxurious life, either. His hotel—a deliberate choice—was no frills and held just the basic bed and shower.

Typically Salim's day began at dawn. He was usually up and out, trying to bring order to the long lines of people waiting to see the three volunteer health care professionals.

Each day the lines grew longer and longer, and the combination of intense heat plus the long wait caused several to faint. The noise of construction didn't help, either. They were in the process of adding rooms to the clinic, and the bulldozing and hammering were deafening.

Salim was actually happier running to the airports or the docks to claim supplies. It was much better than standing in the oppressive heat directing pedestrian traffic. He often used a patois-speaking interpreter to help explain the importance of safe sex.

Over six percent of Haiti's population was said to be HIV positive. There were times he handed out condoms the way the candy man handed out candy. The country had already been blamed for bringing the HIV virus to the United States, and that simply wasn't true.

Still, there was something that compelled Salim to do his part in controlling a virus that had taken far too many lives. Losing a friend to the disease had only reinforced his commitment. The challenge now was to make an uneducated rural population understand the seriousness of the situation. The men simply refused to use a condom, and the women were too scared to insist.

He kept his classes simple and to the point, employing role-playing when he could. Salim often resorted to using fake phalluses and blowup dolls to get his point across.

For the next half hour he and Nate ripped open cartons and unpacked supplies. He took breaks to assist patients filling out forms or when the medical personnel needed help with one thing or another.

"The line's disappeared, bro. You and I have earned ourselves a brew," Nate said, clapping him on the shoulder. "Let's go find a bar in a less depressing area."

"Yeah, I definitely see a couple of Prestiges in our future," Salim answered, wiping the sweat from his face.

Prestige was a local Haitian beer known because it had won a gold medal in the World Beer Cup. It was considered the equivalent of any good American lager.

After checking to see if the volunteers had everything under control, he and Nate headed out to find one of the ramshackle rum shops the locals frequented. By then, they'd been at it for over ten hours and every bone ached.

They hopped into Nate's rented Jeep and navigated around the dancing revelers, arriving at a roadside bar. Music blared from broken speakers. Inside, several locals loudly debated the politics in a mixture of patois and English. There was lots of slapping of backs and loud guffaws. They studiously ignored the arrival of two outsiders. After several attempts to gain the bartender's attention, Nate and Salim were finally served.

Beers in hand, they found a rickety table in the back of the room and made themselves at home.

"So, why are you really here?" Nate shouted over the music. "You didn't think I could handle the project on my own?"

"I have every confidence in you. I just thought an extra pair of hands would be welcome."

"I'm not buying that. You're avoiding something. Is it your old man?"

Salim gulped his beer and set the bottle down harder than he should. "Nah. Not the old man this time. Corporate life was making me crazy. All that posturing and managing personalities isn't my thing. Hell, I was sick to death of being managed myself."

Nate narrowed his eyes. "I thought you'd come to like and respect the woman your father hired. You said you had her checked out and she was clean."

"Clean enough to get into the nunnery. Kennedy had some financial setbacks and a difficult time growing up but that's about it."

"Then what's the problem? Last time we spoke it sounded like you were hooking up."

"She no longer works for TSW."

"How come?"

"She quit."

"Hmmm. Out of the blue? No wonder you're morose. That hasn't happened since you fell for that Senegalese woman who turned out to be married," Nate said sagely.

Salim muttered an obscenity and downed the rest of his beer. "Don't remind me."

"Okay, so you're here licking your wounds instead of pursuing the babe. Why?"

His partner could never just let things go.

"Because Kennedy doesn't want to be pursued. The woman's all about career."

"You're whining like an old lady. Get your uncool self back to Seattle and straighten this out."

"Nope. We're not a good match," Salim said firmly. "Kennedy's a planner. I'm not. She's all about order and I'm the most disorderly person there is. We're different people. I need to move on."

"Whatever." Nate checked out the bar for female prospects and slid off the stool. "I'm going to find myself a hot local girl to enjoy the festivities with. Hey, I may even take her to the cocktail party. Ready?"

He paid the bartender and, popping his fingers to the music, left with Salim in tow.

* * *

Kennedy had been home almost a week when the doorbell jingled. Placing an eye to the keyhole, she spotted a uniformed courier holding a package on the other end.

"FedEx, ma'am," he said. "I need your signature."

She opened the door and he thrust a large white envelope and a small device with a pen attached to it at her.

Kennedy signed the spot he indicated and handed the machine back. She was hoping that the envelope she'd signed for was her last check from TSW. She really could use the money.

The weather had warmed up considerably and she had all her windows open. A fresh June breeze blew through the unit as Kennedy took a seat on the couch and inserted a thumb under the envelope's flap. She withdrew another white envelope with her name scrawled on it.

A check fluttered to the floor as she opened it. Not the company check she expected, but another written from someone's checkbook. The letter accompanying it was written in the same hurried scrawl as the envelope.

Hi, Kennedy,
I'm sorry it's taken me so long to get to you. I heard from several people you were looking for me. I met a man in Seattle and fell in love with him. You know how that is. I asked my best friend,

Summer, if she'd look after your place and collect
the rent. She agreed and then I guess something
happened and she needed to borrow some money.
I am sorry if her behavior caused you problems.
This isn't all the money she owes you but it's
what I was able to get from her. I'll send you
more when I get it. Take care and try not to be mad
at me.
Your cousin,
Marna

It wasn't much money, just a few hundred dollars,
but at least it was something. Kennedy was collecting
rent from the two units, and between that and the
income from TSW, she'd managed to pay down her
debt. Since she'd need to do something about getting
her own car, buying one was on today's agenda.

To date, she still hadn't heard a word from Salim. He
hadn't even called to try coaxing her into coming back.
So much for his pretended interest in her.

That left her to do some serious thinking and start
making future plans. Setting up her own business might
be an option and she'd even drawn up a plan. In the
meantime she needed an income, so she'd listed with a
search firm, and tomorrow she had an interview. She
needed a car.

Kennedy placed Marna's check on her desk and
wandered out to the garden to work. Pulling weeds was

a mindless and relaxing job. She tucked her cell phone in the pocket of an old shirt and went at it. After about an hour spent clearing a garden bed, the phone rang.

"Kennedy Fitzgerald," she greeted.

"I'm glad I caught you at home," a female voice answered. "I know this is last minute but what are you doing for lunch?"

"Who is this?"

"It's Christiane. How are you doing?"

"Hanging in. Taking time off to reflect." Kennedy's curiosity kicked in. Why was Christiane calling her? What was it she really wanted?

"So, are you free?" Salim's sister probed.

"Yes, yes, as a matter of fact. I'd love to have lunch with you. What time and where?" Car shopping could be put on hold until later.

"Some place on the waterfront. It's a beautiful day. If lunch isn't convenient, we could do dinner instead. I can come to Bellevue if you'd like."

"No, lunch downtown is fine. It'll take me less than half an hour to get there. See you in a few."

Christiane's audible exhalation of breath filled her ear. "Good, hopefully this means you haven't found another job yet."

"Not yet."

The conversation veered off in another direction.

An hour and a half later, Kennedy pulled into the parking lot of one of the better-known restaurants on the waterfront. Ray's had been around for ages and drew a diverse crowd, ranging from young adults to people looking for a warm and friendly haven to drink.

Christiane had already secured a primo table on the outside deck. She waved Kennedy over.

"You look nice and relaxed," she said, eyeing Kennedy, who'd let her hair dry naturally. "Being at home agrees with you."

"Thank you."

Outwardly Kennedy might look composed, but inwardly she felt as if she were on a roller coaster ride. Something had prompted this lunch.

"Cocktails!" Christiane said, raising a finger to signal the server.

"Aren't you going back to the studio?"

"Yes, but one glass of wine isn't going to hurt. So, how are you really doing?"

"Keeping busy. Enjoying life. How are things at the studio?"

They were dancing around the issue.

"Not the same since you left. Of course it was mentioned you'd taken advantage of a better opportunity. No one bought that."

"How is Salim?" Kennedy asked, having some difficulty saying his name.

Christiane set down her menu and picked up the drink that had been just delivered. "I don't know. He's in Haiti."

"You mean he walked away from the studio?"

"He said he needed space and time to think."

Kennedy felt as if someone had sucker punched her in the gut. She felt as if she'd fallen down on the job and failed him.

"Who's handling the fall lineup?" she asked. *Please let it not be Leonard.*

Christiane perked up visibly. "Me, while Salim's running away from himself and his feelings. Leonard gives me his input of course, but I'm the one making the major decisions."

"You're enjoying your role, then?"

"Loving it. It's an enormous feeling of power to be able to pick and choose what the American public looks at. I'm actively pursuing getting all these mysterious people off the payroll, the ones Salim mentioned."

"When will he be back?" Kennedy asked, curiosity overcoming discretion.

"Two weeks. Dad's scheduled for surgery again, and Salim promised Mom he'd be back in time."

Kennedy was grateful the server chose that moment to return with their entrees.

"Would you consider coming back to work for TSW?" Christiane asked, startling her.

Kennedy carefully set down her knife and fork. She stared out onto Puget Sound and thought about it. Could she handle seeing Salim again?

"What would I do?" she asked.

"The same thing you did with Salim, help me

develop my leadership skills. I intend to be TSW's next president."

Kennedy loved the thought of a woman in charge. Salim might not return to the studio, so the chances of running into him would be virtually nil. Having a guaranteed income wasn't anything to sneeze at, either.

"Think about it," Christiane cajoled. "Me and you working together, creating an environment to die for and raising that glass ceiling."

"I'm thinking."

"Say 'yes' and I'll make it worth your while. I'll make sure the bonus you were promised happens. I'm all for you having your own show. I'm all for woman power."

"You could hire anyone you wanted," Kennedy said, her stomach fluttering with excitement.

"I want you," Christiane countered. "You know the ropes and the players involved and I need support surviving the world of the good ole boy. You come back and I'll offer a resigning bonus. How soon can you start?"

Kennedy would have to be crazy to walk away from a deal this sweet.

"Tomorrow," she answered, picking up her knife and fork and digging into her food.

"Yeah!" Christiane said, raising her glass. "Yeah!"

Tomorrow would be an even better day than this one was turning out to be. Tomorrow she would be officially employed again.

Chapter 19

"I'm not sure documentaries should be in next season's lineup," Christiane said to Kennedy one evening as they sat in her office strategizing.

"What's the alternative?" Kennedy asked, looking up from her note taking. She'd been working on team-building exercises and had been rolling a number of scenarios around in her head.

She loved working with Salim's sister. They thought alike and were both strategic in their outlook.

Christiane was a natural in the presidential role. She had a nice way with people and a natural aptitude for dealing with some of the more difficult personalities.

She even handled her prickly husband well while making the day-to-day decisions seem easy.

The executive team hadn't outwardly bristled about taking orders from a woman. In fact some had eagerly embraced Christiane's ideas. Yolanda had been one of Christiane's staunchest supporters and Leonard of course was smart enough not to countermand his wife. He'd finally come around to realizing that Christiane had no intention of returning to the role of homemaker, so he'd decided to play along.

Christiane tapped the tip of her pen against her front teeth. "I'm thinking this studio needs a new infusion of sitcoms. Of course the naysayers could argue for a stable and consistent lineup. But if we debuted a select group of documentaries, we could gauge audience reaction and make a decision accordingly."

"You're brilliant," Kennedy agreed. "If you debuted them early, before the competitors' offerings, you'd be able to see the preliminary ratings. We need to wrap up. It's late and your dad's having surgery tomorrow."

Kennedy was dying to ask if Salim was back in town, but she didn't want to appear anxious. She'd been trying hard to forget about him. It just wasn't happening.

Christiane started packing up. She looked up and said innocently, "Salim's back, you know. He flew in late last evening. You might want to give him a call."

Kennedy felt that familiar flutter beginning deep in her

gut. There was a tightening up at the back of her throat that made forming a full sentence virtually impossible.

Did Salim know she was back working at TSW? He must know, yet he'd not called and he'd made no effort to get in touch with her since she'd quit. Who knew what went on in the male mind?

"We need to discuss your talk show. Let's put it on my calendar for when I get back," Christiane said, stuffing a number of folders into her briefcase. "I think having a real life coach share her wisdom would be exciting to an audience. That should beat any dry documentary hands down. We'll debut your show early, too, and see how it does."

It was an exciting prospect, yet Kennedy did not feel that optimistic about it, although having a successful show meant money. She suspected her feelings had something to do with being dumped by Salim because that's what she'd been—dumped.

"I'm heading home," Christiane said. "Heed your own advice and don't stay too long."

"I won't, just another few minutes and I'm out of here. I'll be saying a prayer for your dad and hoping everything goes well for him tomorrow."

"He can definitely use your prayers. Shut the lights off before you leave."

"I will."

For the next half hour, Kennedy lost herself in work. She vaguely heard someone entering the outer room and assumed it was the cleaning people. Even when a throat cleared from the doorway she kept her eyes fixed on the laptop's monitor. Christiane had probably come back.

"What did you forget?" Kennedy asked without looking up.

"My mind, actually," a deep male voice said, making her jump.

Kennedy felt herself go numb all over. She didn't dare look up, not until she gathered her wits about her. She wanted to hurl herself into Salim's arms and kiss him all over.

"You're back," Kennedy finally said, unable to look at him and hoping her voice didn't tremble.

"Yes, I am. I got in late last night after a very delayed flight and hit the hay immediately. Christiane told me you were back at TSW. She loves working with you."

She should have known Christiane would tell him.

"I enjoy working with her, as well." She refused to look at him.

"I'm just glad she was able to do what I couldn't, get you back on board."

Kennedy felt him coming closer. She tensed when he stood behind her. Boy, was she aching to have his arms around her!

The musky, male scent he exuded put her slightly off-kilter. She curtained her lashes and slowly turned toward him. Why did she feel wobbly all over as if she were recovering from the flu?

A loud gasp escaped.

The Haitian sun had turned Salim's skin an appealing cinnamon brown. His teeth were white beacons in his face and his golden eyes were two tawny balls of flashing fire. She wanted to throw herself in his arms and kiss every inch of him, from his boot-clad feet to the unshaven stubble on his chin. She loved the man.

Salim hit the save button on the computer and the system began shutting down.

"What are you doing?" Kennedy sputtered. "I was working."

"No, you weren't. You were trying to figure out how to deal with me."

"I promised Christiane I'd have this project finished by tomorrow."

"My sister is taking the day off. She won't be working." Salim picked up Kennedy's purse and handed it to her. His arm whipped out, anchoring her against him. "You and I are going to have a long-overdue conversation."

When she said nothing he eased her toward the door and began snapping off lights. She should protest and make a huge scene, but what good would that do? There was no one to hear her. She followed him quietly, curious to see where this would go.

Outside in the parking lot, the lights were on and there were few vehicles left.

"You drive and I'll follow you," Salim ordered.

Déjà vu.

"Where are we going?"

"Pick a place where we won't be disturbed."

"I'm going home," Kennedy said with some finality.

Her home was safe and familiar. There she would be in control.

"Home it is, then."

Salim waited for her to get into the Lexus and then shut the driver's door.

"I'll be right behind you," he said calmly, "and I know where you live."

Kennedy's stomach was still in knots when she drove across the bridge to Bellevue. The pickup truck remained never more than a couple of car lengths behind her. What did Salim have to say to her? He played by his own rules and sometimes those rules scared her.

Could he be planning to return to TSW? And could she continue to work for his sister? There was the matter of her bonus. She'd worked hard and she deserved her own talk show.

When Kennedy pulled into her driveway, the pickup truck was right there behind her. She got out, checked her mailbox, and shuffled through the pile of envelopes, anything to delay the inevitable. Marna had sent another scribbled envelope holding a check.

For a brief moment Kennedy thought about the disorder that awaited her. She hadn't picked up the place in weeks. Invitations and decorations for the upcoming reunion were all over the place. In the not too distant past, she would have been horrified to have company, but now she didn't care. There was only so much she could reasonably manage without making herself crazy.

A strained silence descended as she and Salim climbed the stairs side by side. He linked his fingers through hers, but hers felt stiff and dead. What did he want to tell her? Inside, she fluffed the toss cushions and picked up the dishes on the coffee table holding the remains of last evening's snack. She picked up the invitations and put them in a neat little stack, anything to keep busy.

"Come on, sit down and relax," Salim urged when she continued to look for other things to do.

It was her house not his, yet she felt like a guest.

Reluctantly she sat on the edge of the sofa and waited for him to join her.

"I'm here to say I'm sorry," he said, again linking his fingers through hers and squeezing gently. "I've said and thought some awful things about you. I was wrong."

The sincerity in his voice got to her, melting the icicles around her heart a bit.

"I got to know you. I fell in love with you."

He loved her. Those three little words were music to her ears.

"It's more like you hired a detective to check me out and found out I wasn't a cheat," she scoffed, attempting to pull away the hand he was holding.

"What would you have done differently if the roles were reversed?" he asked.

Nothing. As she thought about it, if she'd had the means she would have hired a detective to check out every sordid character her mother had been involved with. It would have saved the family a whole lot of grief.

"It's not a very good feeling to have someone pry into your business and uncover things you would just as soon forget."

Salim's hand cupped her chin. She had that feeling of vertigo again.

"I needed to be sure you weren't some slick opportunist," he said. "I couldn't risk my mother getting hurt. She's endured a long history of my father's philandering."

"Why do you paint such an ugly picture of your father?" she asked, finally relaxing and letting her guard down an inch.

"Because it wasn't an easy life growing up with Tanner Washington, but compared to your upbringing it was a piece of cake."

"I didn't turn out so badly, everything considering," Kennedy said, a smile breaking through. She'd long ago put all that ugliness behind her. Therapy had helped her through.

"You turned out just fine. You're a well-adjusted, emotionally healthy woman and you have compassion. I, on the other hand, had a lot of growing to do."

It was a remarkable admission coming from a man who'd never followed the tried-and-true path.

"Does it mean that you'll be staying in Seattle from now on?" Kennedy asked, holding her breath.

"Not exactly, nor does it mean I'll be retiring, either. I am so mad at what that man did to you. Only a sick SOB would violate a minor. If I were a parent and found out my mate sexually abused my child I'd be in jail."

He wrapped her in his arms, holding on to her as if he would never let go. There was no place that she wanted to be other than here, either. Kennedy laid her head on his chest and let the smell of him engulf her.

"I'm so sorry for what you were put through," Salim said, raining kisses on her eyelids, nose and cheeks.

She'd fantasized about a moment like this. But things had gotten so far off track with them, she'd never thought it possible.

There was still something bothering her. She tried pushing away from him, but Salim held her firm.

"You need to work on improving your relationship with your father," she pleaded. "Harboring all that resentment isn't good for you. Your dislike has become an elephant. It's so big there isn't room for another soul."

"You're wrong, baby. I've already worked through my anger and I returned to make things right. The time away made me think about lots of things. Eventually, I came to the conclusion that I'd never be able to forgive myself if my father passed away and I didn't tell him what was in my heart. In my own strange way I love and admire the man. Look what he built at TSW."

Salim rested his forehead against hers and took several deep, calming breaths. Baring his soul hadn't come easily for him.

In a comforting gesture, Kennedy's arms tightened around his neck.

"Where would you like us to go from here?" she asked.

"I want to give us a shot," he said, staring into her eyes with such raw emotion it almost tore her up. "I can't promise it's always going to be a bed of roses but I'm willing to give a relationship a try."

Kennedy buried her head in his neck. "I think we should definitely give it a try. I'm willing to do at least half the work."

Salim stood abruptly, bringing her up with him.

"I'm not returning to TSW," he said. "Christiane's been doing an awesome job of running the business. She's much better suited to that sort of thing. I'm going to try my hand at producing educational documentaries featuring the work we do at the foundation. Humor me and feature snippets of my films on your talk show."

Salim didn't need her help getting his documentaries in front of a viewing audience, but it was nice of him to ask.

"What about cohosting with me?" Kennedy joked, her fingers kneading his muscular shoulders. "You could be Gayle to my Oprah."

"I want equal billing," Salim whispered, brushing his lips across hers. "In both life and love."

"You have it, babe," Kennedy responded. "And I want…" She whispered something in his ear.

"Me to make love to you? I thought you'd never ask."

Kennedy slowly began unbuttoning her shirt.

"That's my job," Salim said, taking over, and helping her out of it.

He nestled his face between her cleavage. "Yum."

"Come, baby," Kennedy cooed, holding his head captive between her palms.

The next day Kennedy waited anxiously for Salim's call. Tanner's surgery had gone on forever. When her cell rang she wheezed in a breath and picked up.

"How did it go?" she asked.

"I've got good news, babe," he said, sounding happier than she'd ever heard him sound.

"Your dad's operation went well?"

"As well as these things tend to go. His surgeon was pleased with the outcome, and he's resting comfortably.

That's all we can ask. I've missed my favorite girl, though. Want to have dinner?""

"I better be your only girl," Kennedy came back. Even thinking of him as "her guy" felt strange.

Salim's deep throaty laughter sent little shivers skittering up her spine.

"Babe, I love it when you talk like that. Just hearing your voice makes me realize how much I love you."

Kennedy's body still tingled from last evening's lovemaking. Salim had satisfied her in every possible way and afterward they'd talked and talked, holding nothing back.

He'd admitted that it was important to him to have the freedom he needed to continue his work. She'd admitted that having her own business and income was equally as important to her. And they'd agreed that loving each other might mean allowing each other to pursue their individual dreams.

"What are we doing for dinner?" Kennedy asked, forgetting about the team-building exercises she was still working on.

"Chez Washington is always open twenty-four-seven. There are some exquisite carvings the restaurateur picked up in Haiti and he's dying to show off."

Kennedy raised an eyebrow. "You're inviting me to view your etchings?" she asked dryly.

"I didn't think you needed that much urging. Didn't we have a wonderful appetizer last evening? Tonight I get to serve up all four courses."

The thought made a warm tingly feeling envelop her. Later she would tell Salim about the position coaching and mentoring distressed women that she'd been asked to interview for. She loved the idea of doing something useful like helping abused women rebuild their self-esteem.

These were the kinds of coaching jobs that made it all worthwhile, where she could truly make a differ-ence. After completing the test pilot for *Get a New Life*—the name of her talk show—she could devote the time.

"Kennedy," Salim growled, drawing her back to the present. "The dress code at Chez Washington requires you wear only a trench coat."

"The perfect attire for Seattle, rain capital of the world," Kennedy answered gamely.

"And while you're at it…don't put anything on underneath." He lowered his voice several octaves, de-scribing a particularly lurid fantasy.

"Only if you're very nice," she answered, breathless at the vision. "It'll cost you, though. You'll have to attend my family reunion with me. I need a big guy with me in case stepfather number two decides to show up. You never know. Drama follows my family."

"I got your back, babe, always. Don't you worry. But tonight it's party time."

"This is a private matter," she reminded him.

He chuckled, making a shiver skitter up and down

her spine. "Don't you worry. I'm not letting anyone else in on the action. I'll see you in a couple of hours and, uh, no need to belt that trench coat."

"I'm already shutting down my computer," she said, laughing.

"Good. Salmon's in the oven and pinot's on ice. CDs are in the player and I'm already dimming the lights."

She was feeling him completely.

Salim Washington was what she'd always hoped for. She'd needed someone to loosen her up and make her appreciate life. She couldn't let him walk out of her life.

From this moment onward it was the Salim and Kennedy show.

Should she believe the facts?

Essence bestselling author

DONNA HILL

SEDUCTION AND LIES

Book 2 of the TLC miniseries

Hawking body products for Tender Loving Care is just a cover. The real deal? They're undercover operatives for a covert organization. Newest member Danielle Holloway's first assignment is to infiltrate an identity-theft ring. But when the clues lead to her charismatic beau, Nick Mateo, Danielle has more problems than she thought.

TLC—There's more to these ladies than Tender Loving Care!

Coming the first week of December wherever books are sold.

KIMANI
ROMANCE

www.kimanipress.com

KPDH0921208

Too close for comfort…

National bestselling author

Gwyneth Bolton

THE LAW
OF DESIRE

Book #3 in Hightower Honors

Detective Lawrence Hightower's stakeout is
compromised by a beautiful, suspicious stranger.
Minerva Jones needs his protection—but he's not
so sure he can trust her. Minerva is intensely
attracted to the sexy cop, but she's got secrets…
and trouble is closing in.

HIGHTOWER HONORS

FOUR BROTHERS ON A MISSION TO PROTECT, SERVE AND LOVE…

*Coming the first week of December
wherever books are sold.*

KIMANI
ROMANCE

KPGB0941208

Will she let her past decide her future?

NATIONAL BESTSELLING AUTHOR
Melanie Schuster

trust
IN
Me

Playboy Lucien Deveraux is ready to settle
down and be a one-woman man. Trouble is,
Nicole Argonne has no time for "pretty boys"—
especially the reformed-player type. If Lucien
wants her, he needs to prove himself…and
Nicole's not going to make it easy.

"A richly satisfying love story."
—*Romantic Times BOOKreviews* on *Let It Be Me*

*Coming the first week of December
wherever books are sold.*

KIMANI™
ROMANCE

www.kimanipress.com

REQUEST YOUR FREE BOOKS!

2 FREE NOVELS
PLUS 2 **FREE GIFTS!**

KIMANI™
ROMANCE

Love's ultimate destination!

KROM08R

One moment can change your life....

Seduced BY Moonlight

NATIONAL BESTSELLING AUTHOR

Janice Sims

When Harrison Payne sees an intriguing stranger
basking in the night air at his Colorado resort,
he's determined to get to know her much better.
Discovering that Cherisse Washington is the
mother of a promising young skier he's agreed
to sponsor is a stroke of luck; learning Cherisse's
ex is determined to get her back is an unwanted
setback. But all's fair in love and war....

*Coming the first wefi of December
wherever books are sold.*

ARABESQUE®

www.kimanipress.com

KPJS1121208

Love, honor and cherish…

i promise

NATIONAL BESTSELLING AUTHOR

ADRIANNE
byrd

Beautiful, brilliant Christian McKinley could set the
world afire. Instead, she dreams of returning to her
family's Texas ranch. But Malcolm Williams has other
plans for her, publicly proposing to Christian at the
social event of the year. So how can she tactfully turn
down a proposal from this gorgeous, well-connected,
obscenely rich suitor? By inadvertently falling in love
with his twin brother, Jordan!

"Byrd proves once again that she's a wonderful
storyteller."—*Romantic Times BOOKreviews*
on *The Beautiful Ones*

Coming the first wefi of December wherever books are sold.

*Their marriages were shams,
but their payback will be real....*

Counterfeit
Wives

Fan-favorite author
PHILLIP THOMAS DUCK

Todd Darling was the perfect husband…to three
women. Seduced and betrayed, Nikki, Jacqueline
and Dawn learned too late their dream marriage
was an illusion. Struggling to rebuild their lives,
they're each invited by a mysterious woman to
learn more about the husband they thought they
knew. But on a journey filled with surprises, the
greatest revelations will be the truths they learn
about themselves....

*Coming the first week of December
wherever books are sold.*

sepia™

www.kimanipress.com   KPPTD1291208

NATIONAL BESTSELLING AUTHOR

ROCHELLE ALERS

invites you to meet the Whitfields of New York....

Tessa, Faith and Simone Whitfield know all about coordinating
other people's weddings, and not so much about arranging
their own love lives. But in the space of one unforgettable year,
all three will meet intriguing men who just might bring them their
very own happily ever after....

Long Time Coming

June 2008

The Sweetest Temptation

July 2008

Taken by Storm

August 2008

ARABESQUE®